HER SAVAGE
His Heart

In Love With A Miami Bully

3

A NOVEL BY

SUNNY GIOVANNI

© 2017

Published by Royalty Publishing House
www.royaltypublishinghouse.com

ALL RIGHTS RESERVED

Contains explicit language & adult themes suitable for ages 16+

SOUNDTRACK

"Deep" – **Marian Hill**

"Pistols at Dawn" – **Seinabo Sey**

"Heathens" – **Twenty-One Pilots**

"Sledgehammer" – **Rihanna**

"Forgiven" – **Kwabs**

"Famous" – **Kanye West**

"Sleeping with the One I Love" – **Fantasia**

"Dangerous Woman" – **Ariana Grande**

"CRZY" – **Kehlani**

"Trophies" – **Drake**

CHAPTER ONE

It Gets Deep

Ms. Jackson hopped out of her car and ran around the brick wall that covered the trees. Scrappy's home was well secluded and could've been a fortress if he kept the wooden gate to it closed and locked. With a pounding heart, Ms. Jackson stumbled upon Phara on her knees, holding Kalie's hand. When she was close enough, she saw that Kalie's eyes were open. She dropped to her knees in a panic, hoping and praying that the young girl that she had just started to like wasn't done just yet.

"Honey, can you hear me?" Ms. Jackson asked her, patting her hand to make sure that she was aware. "Kalie?"

"Look out!"

Ms. Jackson moved aside so that Scrappy could kneel beside his woman.

"Baby?" he called her. "Say my name, Kay."

Kalie's lazy eyes slowly scrolled from Scrappy to the ceiling.

Lovingly, his hand caressed her cheek, settling against the side of her face to where her ear was between his index and thumb. "Come on, baby. Say my name."

Her lips parted, yet nothing came out.

"Daddy," Phara innocently said with her big and sparkling peepers on him.

Scrappy's head snapped over to her. Just that quickly, he had forgotten that his daughter was present.

Her doll was held tightly at her chest, as usual. "Mama was here."

He flicked his thumb across his nose as a way to keep his rage concealed from his child, yet as the seconds ticked away, it was becoming harder and harder to do.

None of them heard the sirens. Legend had to move out of the way when the paramedics arrived. No one saw him in the doorway to begin with. He just knew that Sheena would be a mess by the time she got to the hospital; just like he knew that Scrappy was about to lose his mind. Within the span of two months, this would be his third trip without him being the one hurt. His boy was at his end.

"Lock up my house," Scrappy told Legend after they placed Kalie on a stretcher. "Ms. Jackson, take Phara back to the shop with you. Make sure she's comfortable."

Everyone followed the orders they were given, and he had to send a text to Calmly once in the back of the rig to tell him to go ahead to Jacksonville.

Kalie's eyes were still open by the time the first responders placed a pressure pack against her chest to help stop the bleeding. Her eyes rolled over to Scrappy, who had his rosary beads clutched between his fingers. She tried to call his name, but her motor skills were a bit off due to how hard she hit her head on the floor when she collapsed. That, in itself, was the only reason she blacked out in the first place.

"Baby," she finally got out.

He looked over at her with softened, reddish eyes that let her know that he was boiling inside.

Without another word, Kalie's eyes rolled into the back of her head.

"It's just the anesthesia," the paramedic told Scrappy.

He breathed a sigh of relief when hearing those words. He thought that he had lost his Kalie.

Sheena, in a complete panic, stepped off the elevator, stomping in her heeled boots to get to someone familiar. Her eyes wildly scanned the empty waiting area, the corridor, and the nurse's station where professionals were laughing and talking about nothing in particular. Finally, she found Legend coming around the corner with his thumb at his chin.

He looked up to see her there, and then spread his arms so that she may collapse within the chest of his white t-shirt. Legend held onto her tightly, feeling her rapid heartbeat against his own. "She's in surgery, baby," he informed her lowly.

"Just tell me that she's going to be alright."

"*No!*" The voice was not from Legend.

Both of them turned around to see a nurse scurrying out of the set of double doors to the operation room, wondering what the hell Kalie could've been screaming for.

"Scrappy! Baby! I want my boyfriend! Get off of me!"

Scrappy stepped up to the doors and placed his hand on the glass, hoping that she could see him and know that he was there.

"She's suffering from delusions!" another nurse shouted so loud that they could hear her. "Give her Propofol."

Scrappy heard Kalie's screams, silently hating himself for not being able to do anything about it. She screamed that "he" was coming to get her, and all it did was make him remember the dream Kalie told him of after she was raped. He should've done something about it to help her heal. Apparently, she was still having bad dreams about it and he wasn't told of it.

"Bro," Legend lowly called him, standing behind Scrappy. "What you want me to do?"

"Find that bitch, and bring her to me."

"You think she's still in Little Haiti?"

"Ain't no chance in hell she's in Little Haiti. Turn it upside down if you got to. I want that bitch found. I'm not bullshittin' with her ass anymore. I love my daughter… but enough is enough."

Without another word, Legend grabbed Sheena by the hand and left the hospital altogether.

Scrappy pressed his forearm into the pane of the doors with his hard eyes on Kalie while she fought on the table; all until she laid back and didn't move again. He ground his teeth while thinking of all the things that he would do whenever Legend and Sheena found Tamara. There was no "if" in the equation. They were boys for life. Where one would pull a trigger for the other, the last two wouldn't hesitate to slice a throat or snap a neck for the first. Tamara might as well had been on the run. After all she had done, she had better changed her name and skipped planets.

———————

Mocha was on her way back to Miami when her phone rang after blocking Dolla from getting through. It was Calmly. An instant smile exploded onto her face. Without a second thought, she pressed the phone icon on her steering wheel to answer. "Yes, sir?"

"Where you at?" he asked her with a low rumble in his voice.

"Driving. Had to clear my head," she responded half honestly.

"You want to go somewhere with me?"

"Like?"

"Jacksonville. I got to work, but I have to clear my head, too."

"What's the matter, Calmly? Got Mocha on your mind?" She smirked when feeling herself a little too much.

"Nah," he chuckled. "I mean, I do, but… it's just a lot going on. Did Sheena call you?"

"About?" she retorted.

"Mocha… Kalie was shot today."

"What?" Mocha slammed on her breaks, almost swerving on the side of the road. "You're joking, right? Calmly, tell me you're joking and this is some kind of sick way that you're trying to get a rise out of me!"

"I wish I was, but I'm not. Phara called Scrap about an hour ago and told him. When we got there, she told him that her mama had been there."

"Where is that bitch?"

"Don't worry about it. Legend and Sheena are taking care of it. Scrap texted me to tell me that Kay is alright. Give me your location."

She took a deep breath, trying to push what she had done and what was going on to the back of her mind. Mocha had more screws loose than her family knew of. "Sunrise," she answered honestly.

"Good. I'm close. Go to the Pilot's gas station on Corinth. I'm going to meet you there in about ten minutes. Maybe less than that."

"For?"

"You're going to Jacksonville with me, woman. That's it."

"Calmly, I don't know who the fu—" Mocha was cut off by the sharp beep that soared throughout her car. She looked down at the display of her GPS to see that he had hung up on her. She ground her teeth until she smirked. He didn't have a problem with putting his foot down with her, and she didn't intimidate him any.

As promised, she parked at the gas station, at a pump though, and leaned against her car with her hands inside her back pockets. An SUV, followed by a solid black, tricked out Mercury, pulled into the station. Haitians and Spaniards alike unflooded the Excursion. Calmly stepped out of his car, blowing smoke from his lips.

He put his Black and Mild cigar out on the rim of the trashcan near the pump where he parked; then he approached Mocha as he took off his white t-shirt. Tucking the remains of his cigar behind the upper piercing of his ear, he pulled Mocha by her hip into a hug.

Fondly, she coiled her arms around his neck and accepted a kiss from his thick lips. "Damn, you smell good," she commented through her astonishment. "What is that?"

"Versus," he responded with a smirk. "You're going to work with me."

She smacked her teeth.

"Nah, that wasn't a question. Shit got to get done while the rest of the family is being taken care of. You're comin'. You wanna fight about it, Mo?"

"Who?" Her face twisted.

"You. *Mo.*"

"My name is—"

"I know what that nigga used to call you, but you're my Mo. So, get ready to work because, regardless, we got to eat."

"Calm—"

"Oh, you thought that this was an opportunity for a discussion? Nah. This is the opportunity for you to fill up your gas tank and follow me." He finally released her hip so that he could pull his wallet from the back pocket of his heavily starched jeans. Then, he pushed and pulled his bank card out of the slot at the pump where she parked. "You want somethin' to eat out of here? We ain't stoppin' again for another three hours; like right when we're close to J-Ville."

She narrowed her eyes at him, loving the way he was so much different from Dolla. Sure, he was rough, but he had her best interest at heart through it all. His attitude turned her on but reassured her that she wasn't alone in anything. She would have to get used to the man that was Calmly when she thought that he was just a boy. There was much more to experience during their unexpected trip.

CHAPTER TWO

Dear Desperado

*S*heena wasn't trying to listen to a damn thing. It took less than an hour to find Bartholomew, Tamara's brother, and hem him up in his own house. She didn't care about the screams of his wife in the background or the fact that his two small children were watching while Legend sat on the couch in their living room with his legs crossed.

With the man who stood only five feet with eight inches to spare against the wall, she wrinkled the neckline of his t-shirt within her fists. Her face was only mere inches away from his. "Where the fuck is your bitch ass sister, nigga?" she asked him through caged teeth. "I know you know where the fuck she is."

"Please, not in front of my kids," he silently begged.

"Fuck them!" she spat angrily. "You know what your niece saw because of that bitch? Tamara hung herself in my brother-in-law's fuckin' driveway! She shot my sister in the goddamn chest, and it was your niece that had to call her daddy to tell him about it! Now, you tell me where the fuck she is before your kids see worse."

"I don't know!" he bellowed, trembling.

Sheena pulled him off the wall, tossing him over the couch where he crashed into his glass coffee table. She was She Hulk when angry, and if he thought that she was close to being done, he was wrong. Sheena didn't have any patience.

Legend lit a cigarette, and then stuffed the box of the remaining singles inside the pocket of his shorts. "Babe," he called her as if the damage she was doing to the living room wasn't affecting him any. "Let me get the kids out of here."

"No!" Bartholomew's wife screamed with wet cheeks. She was clutching both her children at either side of her.

"Look, I done already had one kid who watched her stepmother damn near bleed to death. I don't want no more kids seeing something like that, you got me? Get them the fuck out of here!"

"Please don't hurt him!"

"It's going to get a hell of a lot worse if he doesn't tell my wife where his sister is. You better tell his ass to tell us where she is before you become a widow and your kids don't have a father."

"Tell them! Tell them, Bat! Please!"

"Shay, I don't know!" Bartholomew spat back. "I would've been done told them something. You know that! Moun sa yo mèrdik fou! Tamara se pa sa valè m 'pèdi lavi m' sou. Si ou konnen ki kote li se, jis kouche ak di ou pa fè sa. Mwen pa vle yo touye ou!"

"Really?" Legend asked with a tilted head. "Nigga, my bro is Haitian. You don't think that I would've learned how to speak his language?"

"What did he say?" Sheena asked with her eyes still on her bleeding victim.

"These people are fucking crazy! Tamara ain't worth me losing my life over. If you know where she is, just lie and say you don't. I don't want them to kill you!"

Sheena looked up at the wife with flaring nostrils. "Where the fuck is she?"

"I don't know," Shay told her with a sniffle. "Just give me your number, and I'll work feverishly to give you the answers you need. I swear to God that I will get back to you in less than four hours with her if you just promise to spare my husband's life."

Sheena snapped her fingers for the woman to fetch a piece of paper or her phone so that she could give her a number where she could reach her. Complying, Shay ran into the bedroom to retrieve her charging cell phone, and then handed it over. Quickly, Sheena logged her number and handed it back to her.

"You got four fuckin' hours, and I *will* be back to finish him off. If you think about running, just know that I *will* find you. And if I don't, *Scrappy* will."

Legend lowly chuckled with his smoke seeping out of his nostrils. "Everybody knows how Scrappy is in the dark of night."

Sheena turned away with her heart pounding harder than it ever had. She could barely feel her cell phone vibrating in her back pocket as she tread to the Lexus in her heeled boots. Legend caught her just before she could place her hand on the handle of the car door. His lips fused with hers before she could talk shit or oppose his love.

With he pulled back, he blew the last of his smoke from his cigarette. "Calm down, Desperado," he joked, though she knew he was serious all the same.

"Legend—"

He held up his pointer finger to her, hearing Scrappy's prank ringtone going off in his back pocket. "What's up?... Really?" He then looked at Sheena with his brows rose. "Well, that's unfortunate."

"What is it?" she panicked.

He threw up his pointer finger again, slightly turning to the side to scare her some more. "Damn... I don't know how I'm gonna tell Shee-Shee. That's some heavy shit, dawg."

"What?"

"Yea. We gon' have to start plannin' early and shit and go over life insurance policies real soon."

"What?" she shrieked. Sheena instantly became lightheaded; her body fell numb.

"Aight. I'll holla." When he turned to her with a straight face and shoved his phone back inside his pocket, he looked down at her to say, "She's been in her room for a minute. They stitched her up and gave her a sling for her arm."

Sheena squinted at him, and then slugged him in the chest.

Legend lost all the wind he had left as he stumbled backward.

"What the fuck is wrong with you?" she screamed at him. "Why would you do that to me?"

He coughed, trying to catch what little breath he had left. "Goddamn,

Sheena. Remind me not to piss you off again."

"Don't play like that," she pouted and folded her arms.

"Scrap wants alone time with Kay for now, but he says that we can come tomorrow to see her."

"Is she okay?"

Legend spat out a glob of mucus onto the dying grass around his feet to try and clear his airways. "Yea, she's alright. Just high on anesthetics. Damn, you knocked me in the fuckin' chest. You gon' have to kiss it and make it feel better."

"Kiss my ass." She rolled her eyes and swung the car door open.

"Oh, but I plan on it, with your fine ass."

Kalie grew hot underneath her covers. Her recurring nightmares of Bandz had resurfaced. She was running through what appeared to be an abandoned warehouse when he stepped from behind a pillar. She woke up just before she would have bumped into him. Her back snatched off the sheets beneath her. It took her a minute to take in her surroundings. The room was dark. The only light was over her bed. Just as she turned her head, she was staring into a pair of majestic, blue eyes that told her no lies. Her champion. Her hero.

She didn't even let Scrappy say a word before she tried to reach for him. A sharp pain shot up her left arm and chest. Finally, she realized that she was wearing a sling and a hospital gown. The back of her head began to ache. Kalie used her right hand to reach around and part her hair with her fingers. There she felt the stitches where they had to sew up a whole inch split in her skin where she opened her flesh when hitting her head on the hardwood floor. Tears welled in her eyes as the vision of Phara hovering over her rushed back to her with so much power that it caused her to shiver.

"Baby, you're fine," Scrappy assured her tenderly. "You get to go home tomorrow after they take the staples out of your chest."

"She shot me." Kalie's voice quivered. "Your baby's mother really shot me, Scrappy."

"I'm going to take care of that. Don't worry about her."

"No," she said strongly as her head whipped over to him. "You won't go and get yourself into trouble when you've made it this far."

"Woman, I am sick and tired of her doing shit and getting away with it. I have had enough. I could've lost you—"

"Oh my God." Her eyes diverted to the sheets at her side. "Where's Phara, babe? Is she okay? She… she could be traumatized. I should've never opened the damn door. I should've locked the gate."

"Baby, stop." Scrappy eased onto the side of the bed to wrap one arm around her waist. "Nothing is your fault, alright? Nobody told Tamara to do what she did."

"Scrappy, I can't take this," she sobbed. "I can't take her waiting every fucking chance she can just to try and either kill us or herself. I can't. I don't want to go through this anymore. I'm not going no fucking place. You bring her to me. We need some kind of understanding around this motherfucker because, beyond us, it's Phara having to live through all of this. I will be damned. We've gone through too much as kids, and never do I want her to experience that."

"She won't, baby. You hear me? I'm done with Tamara. I will bring her to you, but it's my hands that her blood goes on. Understand?"

Kalie leaned away from him with a look of discomfort and confusion written across her face. He was more than serious, and his baby's mama didn't have a choice but to accept either punishment. "Scrappy... you're not talking about killing her."

"Oh, but I am." He rose from the bed, wiping his hands down his face as he gathered the right words to let fly out of his mouth so that he wouldn't scare Kalie away. The last time he yelled at her, he had broken her heart. That's not what he wanted, but he had to tell her the truth either way it went. "Kalie, where we come from, it's not always a conversation to be had. I need you to understand that. I am a man who has almost lost his daughter and his woman within a two-month span. I'll be damned if I lose either of you. She's toyed with my time, my money, my loves, my fuckin' freedom, and my sanity."

Kalie locked eyes with him when he finally turned to her. Her tender heart pounded in sorrow and confusion. Could she even open her mouth to try and save a life?

"The reason that I was afraid for you to love me was because she told me numerous times of how much of a bad person I was. She tried her best to convince some of my people and my associates that I just did her ass dirty when I was nothing but good to her. I practically bowed at the girl's feet. When it was over, you would've thought that we were done. Nah. She just had to push and push about how much of a monster I was when all I did was ease her into my world and showed her what I did for a living and how vicious this world could be. She had me afraid of you loving me, Kay. I didn't want you to see whatever the fuck it was that she saw."

"But I do see you, Scrappy," she said no higher than a whisper. She was on the brink of another round of tears. "I know you, and I love all of you. I don't give a damn what she said about you. I know what I've seen and gone through. We have much more to see and experience. Now, I need you to see that for yourself. We have to take care of Phara, and we can't do that if you end up in prison."

"You know how many bodies I've dropped without seeing the inside of a jail cell? Girl, I've only been to county for public intoxication, speeding, reckless driving, and jaywalking tickets."

"Go back. Did you just say—"

"Yea, your man's a murderer, but on black and white, I'm just a regular person. There you have it. You want to walk away now, Kay? Hmm?"

"I hate it when you do that."

"Do what? Tell you the truth and then say out loud what you're thinking?"

"No! When you get so hard with me and try to push me the fuck away like I'm the one who's done something to you. Stop asking me if I want to leave yet."

"I don't want to lose you!" he barked.

"And you won't! Stop flaring up at me when I told you that I'm not going anywhere! I told you that I was staying! I meant that! I told you that I would experience the many layers of you! If you don't ease the fuck up off of me, then you can watch me walk away, Edwin Broadus, and I mean that shit from the bottom of my heart. I'm not the fucking enemy!"

Scrappy pushed his palms into his eyes to calm himself. "I don't want to live in fear. I've done that enough."

"Babe, come here."

Against his better judgement, he let his walls down with her once more and pulled his chair up to the bed so that he could lay his head in her lap.

Gently, Kalie ran her fingers through his locs. She was understanding him a little better. Scrappy was angry and would become defensive when he was in fear. This was probably why Tamara called him a monster all those years. "You don't have to fear me leaving you, okay?" she told him lovingly. "I'm here. I need you to trust that you won't lose me. I love Edwin and Scrappy. I love Phara even more. My place here is sealed and etched in stone. I'm not going. Do you hear me?"

Lightly, he nodded and rubbed the side of his face on the sheets. They were going to have to walk through the fires of hell to officially seal their bond.

CHAPTER THREE

Queenie's Decree

*M*ocha couldn't let her smile leave her face. It was more than obvious that Calmly was her man and he was everything that she had ever needed. For him to put his foot down while leaving her unmoved and submissive had her so open to him that she was willing to do anything that he wanted of her. After spending time with him on duty, she learned to appreciate the "worker bees" as she called them. To see him handling money and product so effortlessly, it turned her on and educated her all the same. Upon returning to Miami, she didn't want to go back to Queenie's. She stayed an entire week with Calmly getting her spine snapped in half and being genuinely appreciated. The feeling was something that she never felt and was something that she had become addicted to within seven days.

Unfortunately, everyone's vacation was over when Queenie called a dinner. They had been skeptical about arriving; especially considering the fact that no one had told their mother or mother-in-law about what had happened to Kalie.

After pushing Mocha's chair up to the head of the table, Calmly took his seat to wait for Queenie like everyone else.

Legend was whispering something to Sheena that made her blush, meanwhile, Scrappy had sent a goofy text to Kalie that made her laugh. She had to use her right hand to slap his arm since him making her laugh hurt her chest a little. He knew that she wasn't fully healed, yet he insisted on her using her arm and chest muscles.

Days prior, Shay let Sheena know that she had a lead on Tamara, which she relayed to Scrappy. She had skipped the state line and had gone to Georgia. They were planning on faking Bartholomew's death just to bring her back for the funeral. Needless to say, everyone's spirits were way up, and there was nothing that could bring them down.

"Isn't this so lovely?" Queenie gushed as Chocolate pulled out Queenie's chair so that she could sit. "Look at all of you in love."

Sheena twisted up her lips, keeping in mind that Legend had told her to keep her cool this time at the dinner table. The last time they were at breakfast, nothing seemed to go right, even after such a magical night. At the opposite end of the table, Mocha casually swiped her blond locks behind her ear and readjusted herself in the chair. None of them had heard from Queenie since that horrible day, so this dinner was a shock.

"Choc, bring in our guest, please?"

After Chocolate turned the corner, Queenie's eyes landed on Kalie's arm in the sling. Her smile faded as she took her eyes to Scrappy, wondering why he hadn't told her of Kalie hurting herself.

Mocha threw a smile at Calmly simply to reassure him that she was trying her best to be nice. Yet, that beautiful smile that he had no problem complimenting faded when she just so happened to turn her head.

Legend and Scrappy stood out of their seats simultaneously, leaving Calmly to follow suit. All three pulled their guns from the back waistbands of their slacks and loaded the chambers to let the so-called guest know that he was one dead man.

"Sons! Sons!" Queenie called them. "Please, put your pistols away. He's our guest. We must treat him as such."

"What the fuck is he doing here?" Mocha managed through gritted teeth. Her chompers were grinding so hard together that she was bound to chip a tooth. Her face read that she was beyond a point of snapping.

Kalie stood beside Scrappy with her jaw ajar and her brows scrunching tightly together. "His brother raped me and you allow him in this house? He's a guest after all he's done to your business? To Mocha? To your sons-in-law?"

"Kalie—"

"Oooh, you've stooped to a new low, Queenie Devieux," Mocha sang with a shaking head.

"And what low is that? I'm looking out for my family. My grandchild deserves their father."

"Your grandchild has a fuckin' father," Calmly told her.

"Yes, I'm sure he does, Calmly—"

"It's a he?" Dolla asked in amazement. "We're having a he?"

"Naw, nigga," Calmly told him strongly. "Me and *her* are having a he. You got a motherfuckin' problem with it?"

"Babe," Mocha called him. She could feel the rage building inside of him. Everyone around the table knew that he wasn't one to refrain from doing anything rash.

"Why did you bring him here?" Sheena angrily asked her mother. "This is disrespectful to everybody at this table. Dolla should be dead by now!"

Queenie squeezed her temple. "Everybody, sit the fuck back down and put your guns away! He's here to discuss business that I'm more than sure can benefit this fuckin' family! The only reason he stands— alive and breathing— is because he is in debt to me, and he can bring in more revenue. With sixty percent of his earnings—"

"Mocha was right," Kalie mumbled. "You haven't found that line between being a boss and a mother. You slapped the shit out of me when you thought that I was pregnant by his brother, yet he can stand here a free man because of money? That doesn't even remotely sound right. I just hope that Mocha wouldn't sacrifice a list of betrayals for monetary gain when it comes to her own child because I know for a fact that there's no fucking way possible that I would let a snake into our house."

Scrappy, still looking at Dolla with his wrist ever so steady while holding his gun, promised, "I would cut its fucking head off if it ever slithered into our house." Then, he placed the safety on his nine millimeter before stuffing it back inside his waistband. "Flockas, let's get the fuck out of here. Apparently, our *mother*-in-law needs to come to her senses. I only pray that she knows what the fuck she's doing."

Mocha kept her eyes on Dolla as everybody filed out of the dining room. She couldn't believe that her mother had the audacity to let such a sneaky and deceitful man into her home. "You better not think of fucking over this family, William," she warned him. "I made you a promise, and you know that I keep my fucking promises."

Calmly interlocked his fingers with hers so that he could pull her out of the dining room. He had other questions that he wanted to ask her, but they would have to wait until they had gotten to his home. He would never reprimand her or try to put her in her place in front of others. His questions were no one's business.

Legend strongly eyed the man as he passed on his way out with his woman in tow.

Queenie was able to grab Kalie's arm before she could pass. "You know that I'm sorry for hitting you, don't you?"

Kalie snatched her arm away from her mother's grasp. "I told you that I was raped. Everybody proved it. You still have yet to ask me of it, but the first thing you put on display when you're able to get us all under one roof is this deceitful motherfucker. Yea, I truly see how sorry you are, *Madam* Queenie."

"Kalie—"

She waved her mother off and was happy that Scrappy pulled her along to get out of the house.

Queenie was at a loss. At the sound of the front doors closing, she plopped down inside her chair and placed her finger at her chin. She was in awe of her family once again walking out on her.

"We'll always be hybrids," Dolla told her at her side. "Half crown, half human. Our responsibility is always split down the middle between conscience and pride. Sometimes, what we see as what's best for the land is not what is always best for our family. It's a great responsibility. I understand you though, Queenie. If there's anybody who's perfectly capable of running Miami on their own... It's you."

"Get your ass-kissing self out of my goddamn dining room."

Dolla bowed his head, but turned away anyhow.

"If you forget my money... or you try to fuck me over... I will waste no time in killing you. You better believe that I'm capable of *that*."

With what pride he had left, Dolla treaded out of the home and ventured to his car. Patting the belly of his white dress shirt, he looked back at the mansion with a clenching jaw. Slowly, a smirk grew up on his face. He had formulated his own plot. Queenie wouldn't be in control much longer. He just needed to earn her trust, and then strike when she was at her weakest. Mocha? He would be seeing her, definitely. He knew how to get her. For killing his brother, she would be seeing him soon.

CHAPTER FOUR

What Have You Done To Me?

Kalie hugged Phara tightly as soon as they retrieved her from Magical's home in Little Havana. She even sat in the backseat with the girl as she slept. Scrappy had to keep looking back at them to make sure that they were okay. Kalie would stroke Phara's locks and look at her with wonder behind her eyes. Scrappy took notice of this and reminded himself to speak up about the things that Kalie could be thinking when spending time with Phara. He knew that she felt bad about scaring the young one, and she felt even worse when thinking of how traumatized his daughter could be after seeing Kalie on the floor bleeding.

When they got into the house, Kalie carried Phara to her bed, where she took off her baby doll flats, her necklace, and bracelet. Purposely, she left her in her short-sleeved t-shirt and undies. Lastly, she removed her denim skirt. Afterward, she kissed Phara's forehead before turning off her bedside lamp.

Scrappy laced his fingers with hers to lead her to her master bedroom. He sat her on the foot of her bed and took off her heels for her. So much he wanted to say, yet he couldn't find the words. His heart was heavy for the Devieux sisters. He knew that they all could handle their own, but it wouldn't be so easy to do when the betrayer was their own mother. To know that Dolla was back in the picture was something entirely different. He and his boys would handle that, including Calmly having to keep a closer eye on Mocha. The look in her eyes said that Dolla scarred the woman deeper than anyone had known, and she was all too angry at dinner for anyone to try and get a read on what the issue could've been.

Kalie tilted her head back at the feeling of her kneeling man, using his massive, rough hands to squeeze and caress her feet and calves. "Baaaabe," she moaned. "God, that feels good."

He didn't return an answer. He was still stuck in his thoughts.

"Scrap, have you given any thought to you and Phara moving in?"

Still, he was so far gone into what he was thinking and feeling that he couldn't hear her.

"Baby?" She leaned up to look at his blank and excelled expression. Kalie waved her hand in front of his face. "Scrappy?"

He blinked only once before he looked up at her. "What?"

Kalie giggled. "I asked you if you had given any thought to you and the baby coming to live here for good?"

"What's this about?"

"It's… it's about us being a family, Scrappy. You, me, and Phara.

Besides that, it's the fact that too much has been done at your house, and that we don't need that bad energy circling around us. She's seen too much there. I think it's in our best interest—"

"You see the little girl that you once were in my daughter, Kay. Be honest about it."

She had no comeback. He had read her and hit the issue dead on the head with a heavy iron hammer.

"It's not a secret. After tonight, it's even more obvious than it was before. Queenie really fucked y'all up. You don't want to do that to Phara, and you don't want it happening to her. Everything that Queenie put you through, you want to be there to block it from happening to my kid. But, baby, nothing will happen to Phara because her daddy has her. Luckily, her daddy chose one hell of a young woman to help raise her."

"Thank you," she mumbled. "One of these days, we're really going to have to sit down and talk."

"Enough of that for now. Bend that ass over." He pulled her up by the hand, bending her over the bed. Eventually, he would have to stop pussyfooting around the issues.

"Can you believe her?" Mocha was still fuming after Calmly allowed her a glass of red wine to help soothe her nerves. She wouldn't stop pacing in her cocktail dress with her bare feet pattering against the hardwood floor of his bedroom.

He sat on the foot of his bed, as content as he'd ever be, with his X-Box controller in his hand. Even though he seemed as if he wasn't listening, he hung onto her every word. Only in his briefs and dress socks, his eyes were hard on his screen while halfway enjoying his NBA 2K for the night.

"She let him into the house after he tried to take her entire fucking empire."

"Mo, sit down." His voice was hardly inaudible over the sound of the roaring crowd from his surround sound system.

"This motherfucker is up to something. I know him."

"Mo…"

She swung her arm outward, almost spilling what little wine she had left in her glass. "Nooobody is supposed to listen to me, are they? No, of course not. It's because I'm the crazy bitch. I'm the evil enchantress that can't stand to see others better themselves."

"Mo!" Calmly paused his game to look at her with a raised brow. "Man, sit the fuck down somewhere and stop worrying about that bitch ass nigga. Do I look concerned to you?"

"Calmly, he—"

"Do… I… *Look*… Conceeeerned?"

"But—"

"Sit… your ass… *down*."

She smacked her teeth with her eyes rolling, but she sat down on the side of his bed anyhow.

Calmly placed his controller on the top of his glass and iron entertainment set, and then rolled over to lay across her lap. "You mad?"

"Leave me alone," she told him with a pout.

"You need to calm the fuck down before this baby comes out with six fingers and four toes."

"Don't think I didn't hear you say that my baby already had a father. How can you be the father, when—"

"My name is Carlito Don Cortez; my birthday is December 4th, 1995. Favorite color is black, favorite food is Mexican pizza, and I love anchovies. Anything else, Michelle?"

"Don't get popped in the mouth."

"What else you want to know, since you're trying to deny me my rights?"

"Your rights?" she snarled.

"Yeah. Straighten your face."

"Excuse me?"

Calmly grabbed her jaws. "You heard me, girl." Gently, he pulled her face down to his for a kiss that he knew would shut her up and have her quiet for a very long time.

"Calmly?"

"What, Mo?"

Playfully, she smacked his cheek and pushed him off her lap. "Stop thinkin' you can run me, boy."

"What I tell you about callin' me a boy?"

"You gon' get off the floor?" Mocha crawled to the foot of the bed.

He was lying there on his back with a smile on his face, exposing his whole row of bottom, gold teeth. "You gon' come down here?"

"No." Mocha concealed her smile. "You come up here."

His phone rang near his controller, disturbing the moment. Calmly reached up to answer it with a grimace. To keep her temper at bay, Mocha focused on the tattooed, fully blossomed roses on his right hand.

"What's goin' on?" he grumbled, sliding his free hand up the ripples of his abs. "Nah, I'm at the crib. You was thinkin' of comin' over?"

Mocha tilted her head at him. She was dangerously close to telling him something about himself if he was talking to another female.

"Let me go and unlock the door then."

"Unlock the door?" Mocha scoffed.

"Oh, that's my old lady."

"Old lady, Carlito, really?"

His golden cheeks became rosy. "Let me let you in."

"Let who in?"

Calmly rose from the from the floor and rummaged through his drawers to find a pair of basketball shorts to throw on.

"Calmly... don't play with me right now. Who the fuck are you letting into the house?"

He didn't respond. He went about his duty to travel down to the first floor of his home, and then to the door that he had no issue in snatching open.

Ireful, Mocha stomped out of the room so that she could lean over the banister with a tall back like the empress she was.

A short woman stepped through with her brown face reading that she was not at all happy. Her short bob complemented her age. Mocha inspected her salt and pepper strands, calculating that the woman was in between the ages of forty and fifty years of age.

"I haven't spoken to you in a week," she complained in Spanish. "Here."

The woman pulled a young boy into the house by his shoulder, shoving him into Calmly's leg.

"Hey!" Calmly gushed as he picked up the little brown-skinned boy who wore his hair in a mohawk with golden, frosted tips. "Did you miss tío? You said you did over the phone."

"Have you spoken to your wretched sister?"

"No, Madre."

"Carlito, I'm tired. This is driving me insane. I was done raising kids—"

"When you were done raising me. I get it. But you keep in mind that you never raised me. You never raised any of us. I help you with Samuel. I give you three grand, just to support him."

"Your money means nothing to me. You find that girl and make her take care of her responsibility. Now, he said that he missed you, you got to see him, and now, I have to take him home to sleep. He has to go to that school for special needs boys tomorrow. Do you know how embarrassing that is?"

"Embarrassing? Can you not hear how you sound? Don't say things like that in front of Samuel."

"Well, it is."

"And it's my money that pays for his schooling, so I said don't speak about him like that."

"I would let you keep him, but you have a lot of problems of your own, like dodging both heaven and prison. Give him to me."

The woman reached for the boy, and an ear-bleeding screech came out of him. For a moment, it was like a push and pull match to gain him in their arms. Finally, Calmly's mother won the match, cracking a piece of Mocha's stone heart as she watched.

Calmly kissed his nephew's forehead and closed the door when his mother was far away from the porch for him to even see her. When he turned and saw Mocha up behind the banister, he said, "I wanted him to meet you. He asked me who you were when he heard you in the background." With a straight face and a very calm demeanor, he locked his front door, and then marched up the steps to his bedroom without another word.

His woman stood there, fortunate to have the demoness that she knew to be Queenie as her mother instead of the mean and ungrateful witch that birthed her boyfriend. She was going to have to get with her sisters to speak on these issues because Queenie may have messed them up as children, which spilled over into their adult lives, but they needed to get over the scars together.

CHAPTER FIVE

What I Get For Loving You

Dolla hung his head before getting out his car. He had a lot of time to think over everything that he had done. The fact that he was a made man who now had to bow at someone's feet was beyond him. Over that, it was the fact that he had a burned image in his mind of how defensive Calmly had gotten over Mocha. It should've been him at the table looking after his woman. Instead, it was a man that he had hired to be his muscle. She looked so comfortable. So beautiful. Her smile warmed his heart, even though he had the intention of going in there to dinner to intimidate her and to remind her of the shit she talked to him about killing his brother.

Mocha was a real piece of work. His piece of work. How could she even just leave him, go to the extent of trying to kill his brother, and then hook up with someone who he considered beneath him? Had he really hurt her that badly?

Dolla pushed all these thoughts to the back of his mind and pushed through to get out of his luxury car. With it nearing one in the morning, he had already gone to the club where he started out of. At seventeen, he had strong armed the owner to let him sell his variety of products inside. For three long years, he was able to triple his income that way. Tonight, he proposed that he start up again. Surprisingly, he didn't have to force anything. The owner thought that it would be a good business venture to have more people to fill the space. Queenie couldn't make everybody blacklist him.

Through a modest door, Dolla had gone and found Tamara sitting on the couch in the living room of the one-story abode. He shook his head at her and traveled down the hallway to the room in the corner just before getting to the master's suite. After opening the door, a smirk appeared on his face.

"Baby brother… Don't look so glum."

Bandz stared out of the window from the chair he sat in. For the last few weeks, he was concealed in darkness. Dolla knew not to turn on the light. His brother would always make it seem as if he would have an allergic reaction to it.

"You still in your pajamas, or did you change before I got in?"

Still, Bandz didn't returned a word.

Dolla sat on the side of the bed, pulling the legs of his jeans up. "I told Mama that I would take care of you when you were sixteen. I never broke my promise. I might have been very brutal with you, but that's because I wanted better for you. So, believe me when I say Mocha's a dead bitch for what she did to you. Just let me get my namesake first."

"These bitches are poison." Bandz's top lip rose with disgust. "She took my manhood away from me, Dolla. She just… took it."

"At least she didn't get to take your life away from you. Had

34

Tamara gotten to you an hour later, you would've been gone. I just thank God that you're a slow bleeder."

"Don't act like you give a fuck about me when you're not the one who had to have surgery to get your junk reattached. You're not the one who had to lay there and have a nurse— while getting blood transfusions, by the way— try to stimulate you while you're in severe fucking pain."

"But you can still get it up, can't you?"

Bandz finally took his eyes away from the window to pry through his brother with them. "Motherfucker, I get erections just because the wind blows. That bitch did this to me. She did this to me, and because of it, my dick won't ever be the same. She came within inches of fuckin' killin' me. So you know how I feel, *Will?* Fuck Michelle, fuck Queenie, fuck Kalie, and most definitely fuck Edwin for stealing my girl and my kid. He probably knew all this time that Mocha was gonna come for me. I know how to get him back, though. I'm going to make sure that he knows that he can't have both my kids. He already got Phara, but he ain't takin' my unborn."

"About that…" Dolla rubbed his chin. "At dinner… Kalie didn't look at all pregnant, bro."

"It's still early."

"She has a washboard, like she's always had."

"It's *still* early."

"Alright. If you say so." Dolla stood and stretched. His bed was calling his name. "By the way, you didn't tell me that you raped Kalie."

Bandz snarled at his brother. "Who told you that?"

"She told Queenie."

"That's bullshit. I made love to her."

"Yea, okay. Oh, and you might want to do something about Tamara staying here. If Scrappy had half a right of mind to follow me, the both of you would be dead. You need to ask her if she told Scrap that Phara ain't his yet. I told you to look out for that girl; just like I told him that she ain't shit."

"Dolla… get the fuck out of my room, man."

He smirked as he shook his head. His plans were already in motion. His little brother had better find something to do with his life before any of the Flockas wise the hell up and come after him.

CHAPTER SIX

Hold On To Me, I'm A Little Unsteady

A week went by with the girls all being in their feelings about Queenie's decision to let Dolla into the circle. Money was fine for a reason, excluding all of what he had done to them and how he tried to snatch Queenie's kingdom away from her. On a Saturday, they made the decision to link up since they had all been busy with trying to pick up where they left off when Dolla's appearance threw everyone off kilter. That left the men alone to do whatever it was that they needed to do.

Legend went with Calmly to the barbershop, while Scrappy stopped by Ms. Jackson's to have his locs re-twisted. He walked into the shop with a bounce in his step, ready to shock the hell out of Kalie when thinking of having his tips dyed red this time. He needed her to feel something. Anything besides the worry of Phara or the anxiety of waiting for the call from Legend and Sheena saying that they have officially found Tamara.

With a smirk, he greeted the receptionist and passed the women who were getting their weekly dos on either side of the dark green and white checkered floor. Scrappy was a piece of meat that the regulars had been salivating over since he was sixteen. Finally reaching Ms. Jackson's chair, he wrapped his arms around her waist and rested his chin on her shoulder, staring at himself in the mirror.

The woman in the chair was wearing shades. He couldn't tell that the thin woman, who looked like she was out of place in her designers and flawless makeup, was staring at him.

Ms. Jackson, however, looked more than shocked to him. She had completely frozen in place. Usually she would have a quip for him over how disrespected she felt when he would hold her in the manner he was. He eventually caught on and leaned back with his head tilted and his lids lowered.

He asked, "You okay, today?"

Stephanie whisked past him, grabbing his hand in that instant to pull him to her chair that a client had just gotten out of. Scrappy took notice of how she seemed to shiver while getting her tools together so that she could unbraid his ponytail and mix her dye.

"Red, right?" Even her voice shook when asking her question.

Scrappy folded his arms over his chest to keep himself content. Something was off inside the shop. Very off.

Stephanie couldn't seem to get herself together. She rounded the chair with her rat-tail comb and stuck the thin tip of the tail between the crossing of his locs. Scrappy grabbed her wrist behind his head and held a strong eye connection in the mirror. She had better start talking.

Needless to say, Ms. Jackson did one hell of a job when teaching her daughter not to lie or hold secrets. Stephanie looked over at her mother with a shaking bottom lip. In turn, Ms. Jackson looked at Scrappy's reflection in the mirror.

"What?" He was becoming irritated. It was in the tone of his voice.

Ms. Jackson gulped, turning her client's chair around to face him. "Edwin... meet Judeline. Li se manman ou."

Scrappy didn't even blink. He gulped. "My Haitian-Creole is the least bit rusty, but you have to forgive me. It sounded an awful lot like you just said that she was my mother. Am I correct? Did I somehow miss the punchline somewhere? Am I translating that incorrectly? Did you just really say that this woman, who looks like she belongs in Hollywood, Florida, is my mother?"

The woman removed her shades to show Scrappy his exact same eye-shape and color. Her majestic blue orbs spoke the truth. She was in fact a part of his bloodline somehow. She could have been his mother.

Scrappy leaped out of the chair and headed to Ms. Jackson's office. He paced inside, trying to keep his temper at bay. This woman... she looked so much like him with feminine features. He racked his brain, trying to remember what his mother even looked like. His father had destroyed all of her photos and clothes. He never spoke of her outside of the fact that she was a spiteful bitch for leaving. With as much as he had on his plate, he couldn't deal with this.

"Edwin," a soft voice called behind him, followed by the low sound of the door clasping shut. "Edwin, I had to come find you."

Scrappy sucked in a breath to say something when he sharply turned on his heels, but he collected his words and held them inside. Her presence made him revert to choosing not to say anything at all. Had he spoken out of anger, he would've mixed French, Haitian-Creole, and English all into one. She wouldn't have been able to understand him.

"I understand if you don't have anything to say to me. I completely agree with you if you're angry. I just had to see my son. Your twenty-third birthday is coming up, and I figured—"

"Eighteen years," he cut her off with a low rumble within his baritone. He was not at all happy. "You decide to come back after eighteen years? Do you have any idea of what the fuck I went through with the man you married and never officially divorced? You weren't there to accept the lashes! You weren't there to keep him from knocking me unconscious! He starved me because of you! All the money halfway went to rent while the other half went to rum. Where were you?"

"I was—"

"Where?" he shouted.

Judeline flinched, backing up a little. "I... I was in Jacksonville."

He turned away and grabbed his mouth to keep from swearing any further.

"A friend of mine... her son took a picture with you and posted it to his Instagram account. She was teaching me how to work my own when she showed me his account. I asked him about you, and that's when he told me that they call you Scrappy, and that you live in Little Haiti. Edwin, I've missed you."

"Don't lie to me," he told her quietly. "Don't stand to my back and lie to me, woman. You know nothing of me. You don't know who I am. You don't know what the hell I went through because of you. Yet, here you are to try and say that you missed me when all you had to do was come home to see me."

"Angelica Jackson says that you have yourself a good girl." She tried to change the subject, adding a light giggle at the end. "She says that I have a beautiful granddaughter that she sees every weekend. I love what she's done to this place. To convert her old house into a shop is amazing. I remember what it looked like before the conversion. Women would line around the block just to have their hair done on a Friday."

Scrappy's eyes watered. After all the years that he blocked her out, she was there now. He didn't know whether to rejoice, scream, curse some more, or knock her on her ass to make up for all the beatings that he had gotten. He chose wisely by tearing away from the room altogether. He felt like he couldn't breathe as he marched out of the shop. He had to get to his sanity. He had to get to Kalie and Phara just to make everything better.

Kalie lounged poolside behind Scrappy's home while Phara and Sheena enjoyed the water. Mocha sat directly beside her sister with her glass of sweet tea in one hand and the other over her belly.

"I can't wait to have him," Mocha said with a smile. "Calmly would love it if we were having a boy."

"Why are you so hell-bent on having a boy?" Kalie responded

with a giggle.

"Because I think he would be so adorable. I can put him baseball, and I might even have a little surfer. You never know. If I have a girl, she would be just as rotten as me."

"You can say that again."

"Nuh uh. Don't you agree with me. And what about you?"

Kalie lowered the frame of her shades to the edge of her nose just to peek at Mocha over the rim. "What about me, Mocha Latte?"

"You and Scrap hump like damn rabbits. Don't say you don't. When am I getting a niece out of you?"

"Pffsst! You can most definitely wait for that. You already have Phara, even though I didn't birth her."

"Yea, she's cute, spoilable, and she's very intelligent… but I want one that looks just like you. At least then I can make up for time lost."

Kalie had to stare at her sister for a moment. "Lady, my sister would never admit to something like this. Where the hell is Michelle Devieux?"

"Bitch, I'm sitting right next to you." Mocha's phone rang beside her on the glass table Scrappy decorated his poolside with. She saw who was calling and rolled her eyes at it. Of course, she wouldn't have opened her mouth to her sister just to let her know that it was Dolla stalking her phone.

"Mocha, I never got to tell you that I knew something about you?"

"Like what?" She rejected the call and set it on the table as if nothing at all had happened.

"I know that you slept with Bandz."

Mocha froze. All she could do was stare at her sister, anticipating a reaction. How could she have known? A spineless, fragile bitch like Bandz wouldn't have come out of his mouth and told her.

"Before he raped me…" Kalie cleared her throat and repositioned herself in the chair so that she was sitting up to stare at Phara and Sheena in the pool. "He was trying to convince me that you didn't mean anything to him."

"Because I didn't. He didn't mean shit to me either, but that still doesn't excuse the fact that I did it. I was so jealous of you, Kay. You're pretty, you're smart, you went off to college—"

"You're beautiful, smart, and it's still not too late for you to go to college. It's no reason to be jealous of me when you're the same. We just react to things differently."

Mocha relaxed in the chair, feeling bad about what she had done. Usually, she was a woman who didn't regret a thing. She wondered where her sudden conscience came from.

Just the thought of school made Kalie grab her phone from the table beside her and open her email to find an old colleague of hers. She didn't have his number, but she knew his email address was there.

"*Hey you,*" she sent. "*I'm trying to start my own practice, but I want it to be legit. Does it seriously look like I have to go back to graduate school?*"

"Kay!" Scrappy roared from the inside of the house. He was so loud that it shook the walls and made all the girls flinch and turn as if he was standing behind them all. "Baby, where are you? I need you!"

In a hurry, Kalie hopped out of her chair and dashed into the house to meet him in the hall where the bedrooms were. His back was against the wall, his fingertips were digging into his skull, and his chest was rising and falling with a quickness. If Kalie didn't know any better, it looked like he was having a panic attack.

"Baby?" Slowly she approached him. Scrappy was close to either lashing out or breaking. She feared that it was both.

Gently, she caressed his cheeks and rubbed his pierced earlobes softly with her index and thumbs to try to calm him.

"Tell me your name," she instructed him lowly.

For a moment, the only thing in the hall that was audible was Scrappy's heaving.

"Come on, babe. Tell me your name."

"It's… Edwin… Edwin Broadus," he responded though he didn't know why.

"Your favorite color is…?"

"Babe—"

"We can take baby steps or either we can jump right into the big shit. Which do you prefer?"

"She came back," Scrappy suddenly blurted, then ripped away from Kalie to enter into his bedroom.

Kalie followed, just as confused as ever.

"She, up out of the blue, showed up to Ms. Jacksons! How could she leave for eighteen or nineteen motherfuckin' years, and then come back like I was going to accept her tramp ass like she didn't walk away from us, leaving us high and dry?"

She gulped while watching her man pace at the foot of the bed. Scrappy had done something that he had never done. He made her fear him.

"She leaves my old man to make him beat me and fuckin' starve me, and then she comes back? Fuck that bitch!"

"Scrappy!" Kalie called him. She had to put on a brave façade just so that he wouldn't go from being angry to fearful of her leaving him too.

He stopped dead in his tracks, about-faced to her, and then sat on the foot of his bed with his eyes on the floor.

"Can't you see?" she asked him. "I just had a shocking realization about why you put up with Tamara and why you wanted Phara to have both parents. You told me that you were a killer, and I wish you would've heard how you said it because you could've gotten rid of your baby's mother a long time ago. Your mother is the reason. She's the root to the issues. We just had a breakthrough, babe."

Scrappy looked up at her with a frown.

Kalie flailed her arms when pulling off the largest yet fraudulent smile as she approached her love. "Scrap... come on. Look at it like you're facing your demon head on." Then, she took a seat beside him, pulling his head over into her lap. "You can ask so much about why she left. Through her, you can even get an understanding about your old man. Together, you guys can heal."

Scrappy reached for her hand as his own trembled. When he grabbed it, he brought it to his lips and kissed it. Though he wasn't a vulnerable man, he allowed himself to be so open with her. She wouldn't wrong him or hurt him. He knew that his Kay would only make him better. He had long convinced himself of that.

"Baby, is that something that you would be interested in, if I help?"

"Only you," he finally replied. "Right now, I'm not ready though, babe. I'm not ready. I'm pissed the fuck off, I'm hurting and I don't know what's going on."

"It's going to be okay, Scrap." A thought dawned on her in that moment. "Don't you have to meet with the guys soon?"

"I just want to stay home."

"Scrappy, you have to work. There's too much going on for you to crawl inside your shell."

"Kay... baby... I'm really hurting right now, and my head is fucked up. I'm going to—"

"Come unhinged? Fall apart? Become sporadic?"

"I'm not joking."

"I never said you were, babe. I'm just saying that I know you, but I need you to hold on and carry on. Maybe you need a day for yourself. But... that day will have to be tomorrow. Until then..." Kalie softly kissed his ear. "Just know that you are loved..." Again, she pecked his ear. "Without the past, it wouldn't have made you into the overprotective, loving man that you are today. And I love you, Scrap. Nothing bad will ever come to me or, most importantly, Phara because you don't want her to go through the same things. Thank them for the bullshit, baby, and remember that the past is behind you. You're much more than that."

"Kalie, I swear to God, I love you, babe."

"So, that's a yes? You'll sit down with her?"

"I will. But I'm going to take her ass to the asylum so she can see what the hell she did to us all. She's going to have to see her husband."

Kalie knew that the issues were far from over, and she prayed like crazy that she would be able to wrangle the group because Scrappy was not the son that either of his parents remembered.

CHAPTER SEVEN

Where Did You Come From?

Mocha was leaving her doctor's office with the only thing on her mind being that she was going to meet her man for brunch. She wanted a carved watermelon that was in the shape of a bowl, which housed other smaller fruits. Her mouth watered for it. Being six months pregnant now, she and Calmly decided to create their own little routine since Mocha didn't want him to come to her appointments with her. For the last few days, she hadn't been feeling well. She had been experiencing serious nausea and abdominal cramps. Her doctor simply told her that the baby was trying to make room. Today, however, she panicked a little when the nurse had to turn the volume up on the ultrasound machine. Her baby had a very faint heartbeat, and it alarmed her. She feared that someone was misdiagnosing her, but she didn't want to face that.

Before she could get to her car, she checked a message from him that made her smile. She trotted to her car with a hitch in her step when seeing that he basically sent her a page full of beautiful words before telling her of how much he cared for her. Dolla would've never done that.

When thinking of the devil, she lifted her head to see how far she was away from her car when she saw him parked right next to her beautiful Mercedes. Mocha's nostrils flared. "What the fuck do you think you're doing?"

Dolla flicked his thumb across his nose as he leaned away from Mocha's fine, luxury vehicle. "I had enough of your games, Mocha Latte. It's time that you come back home to daddy."

"Move your ass away from my shit, man." She rolled her eyes while continuing her walk to the driver's side door. "You've been trying to hit me up, and I guess since you're blocked, you finally wanted to make an appearance."

"You think I'm playin'? You're mine, Mocha. You don't go around ignoring me and shit and expect me not to pull rank. I let you get away with fuckin' over my brother, but you ain't gonna get away with givin' my seed to another nigga. It just ain't gonna happen like that. I should drop you where you stand, but—"

"But what?" she shouted. "What, Dolla? You love me? You're holding back because you think about all the good times we've had and all the things that we could do as a family? If it is, then you need to drop yourself because all of that ain't what you're going to get from me."

"So, you gon' sit here and tell me that he's better than me?"

"You're green with envy, Dolla. If I were you, I would back the hell away from my car and let me go about my business."

"You gon' have one hell of a custody battle—"

"Can't fight for custody if you're dead, William."

"I only let you get away with *threatening* me, Michelle."

"That wasn't a threat at all. I just have to rethink my plot because you're my mother's boy now. But don't get too comfortable. My man has no problem in takin' your ass out before I do."

"Oh, so he's your man, now?"

"That's exactly what he is."

"Or so you think."

Successfully, Mocha shoved Dolla out of the way and snatched her car door open.

"Aye, Michelle! When you're done playin' with him… You know where to find a real man."

Flustered, hungry, and fed up, Mocha threw her large handbag and phone over into the passenger's seat, and then stepped out of the wedged heels she was wearing. "What'd you say?"

"Oh, so now you're ready to fight?"

"You forgot three things before you let that bullshit fly out of your mouth." Tears welled in her eyes at that moment. She wanted so badly to feel his blood on her hands, yet she knew that Calmly would have a fit if she stressed too much, let alone commit murder, which is why she kept what she did to Bandz under wraps. "One, you were only worth five hundred thousand after expenses when I met your ass. *I* built you up and got you over that million-dollar mark. Two, you could barely wipe your own nose had I not provided the tissue. Dolla, I had to hold your hand when you needed to re-up or buy hoes. That was *me*. I kept your fuckin' books and stashed money for your rainy days. Lastly, don't you ever come for a bitch's nigga when he slaved his ass off from the time his family landed in this fucking country. Let's not forget that, unlike *you*, Calmly doesn't need my goddamn help. Real man? Yeah, I finally got one. One who doesn't have me out here lookin' a fool and would choke the fuck out of me if my blood pressure went up over a single digit beyond the normal rate. So, fuck you, *William*. What I got is real, and I don't need to explain this shit to you."

"So… why are you crying?"

Mocha hurriedly swiped away the gloss from her cheek as she hardened her face. "It's because I'm mourning you before I kill you." With that, she slid into her car, slammed the door, and then started the car to peel off.

While on the freeway, her phone chimed in the seat. She was only lucky to grab it, peak at it, and find that Calmly had sent her one last text.

"*Come home,*" it read.

Mocha obliged. Fuck the food, Dolla, and how badly she wanted to get rid of him for playing her like a fool and all. She just wanted to get home to her man and have him to take everything away.

———————

After a while, she reached Calmly's Little Havana home and rushed through the doors with her stomach cramping. She, first, had to check her makeup to make sure that it wasn't smeared. She didn't need Calmly beasting on anybody just yet. Then, she took deep breaths to soothe the pain she felt in her stomach. She reminded herself that the doctor told her that the baby needed room. Maybe that was what it was. She hung on to that.

Soon after, she sashayed up the steps and into the master bedroom. As soon as she entered, Calmly snatched her by the waist and fused their lips together.

"What was that for?" she asked out of breath.

Calmly bit his bottom lip while looking over her gorgeous, chocolate mounds. He considered himself a lucky man to have the baddest bitch in Miami with the street smarts and business savvy to match.

"I missed you," he whispered close to her lips with passion in his eyes.

Though he made Mocha blush, she didn't have time to live in the moment. He picked her up by the backs of her thighs, wrapping her legs around his waist.

"You haven't been feeling well lately, so I'm going to make you feel better. I'm gonna make love to you, while it's still early, and the sun's still out."

"Are you trying to tell me something, Carlito?" she asked with a beaming smile that she couldn't pull away from.

"Ain't no tryin'. I said it. I love you, Michelle."

Mocha covered her mouth as tears gathered in her eyes once more.

"You blessed me, baby. Now I'm gonna bless the fuck outta you."

"I love the sound of that."

Calmly pressed his lips against hers as he led her over to the bed to sit her on the edge. Then, he took her purse away from her hand to gently sit it on the floor. "How did the appointment go?" Carefully, he pulled her thighs apart and ran his hands along her flesh.

Mocha hesitated while loving the feel of his hands. She couldn't tell him that she ran into Dolla. "It was well, actually."

"Really? What did they say the fatigue and pain was from?"

She shrugged. "They said the baby needed room."

"What did they say about the baby?"

"He's a big one."

Calmly looked up at her with a sparkle in his eyes. It was something that he wasn't telling her, but he would have to eventually. "Really?"

"He's growing at an alarming rate, too. I've gained nearly ten pounds in the last two weeks. Let them tell it, it's normal and it's important for me to gain weight now. I'm headed into the third trimester."

"You're still beautiful, baby." He kissed Mocha's stomach.

"Don't make me cry, Carlito," she whined.

"I'm just happy, baby."

Mocha stroked his sideburn while he kissed the height of her belly.

"Riker. We should name him Riker."

"Or something Spanish," she suggested. "What about Julián? Julián Riker Devieux?"

"Hyphenate that and you got a deal."

"You tryin' to tell me something else, Carlito Cortez?" she blushed.

"Ain't no secret that I'm cuffin' you. We have to do it before Riker's born, though."

"Umm… I don't have a ring." Mocha shook her left hand in the air.

"Be patient. You know it's coming."

Gently, Calmly lay her back on the bed to explore her lips some more. Shortly after, Mocha would feel a familiar pinch as Calmly slithered his manhood inside of her.

CHAPTER EIGHT

When Your Heart Wants To Leave

Kalie had already seen Phara off to preschool and had taken her first two clients for the day over the phone. Since she was at Scrappy's for the week, she wouldn't dare to invite any of them over to his home. Speaking of Scrappy, he was in Jacksonville the night prior and was due back at any given moment. All she wanted to do after a restless night without seeing him was to cuddle up and take a nap. To her surprise, while logging her notes, her iMessage popped up at the corner of her laptop from one Justin Langston. It brought a smile to her face. For a while, she and Justin had been corresponding about school and the things they used to do when she was on campus. He really had her leaning towards going back just to finish so that her practice wouldn't be at all illegal.

"*Going to Facetime you*," he sent to her.

Kalie didn't have to respond before the snapshot of his current position popped up on her screen. She hurried and pulled her tresses over her shoulders, hoping that they wouldn't look matted at all. After readjusting herself in her desk chair, she put on a smile and answered.

Her greeting was stuck in her throat when he looked up at her with his dazzling, pale brown eyes and gave her the smile that made most girls melt on campus. His long, pearly whites gleamed at the screen, having his dimples to sink into what appeared to be just a handsome, muscular face at first. His high yellow complexion gave his blush away when his cheeks turned pink.

"Hello to you too," he chuckled. "It's been a while."

"Nine months," she lowly replied.

"God, you're still gorgeous, Kay. Are you still on your Spartan diet?"

"One meal a day with eight mile runs," she responded atop a giggle. "Sometimes, yes. How about you?"

"Have to keep fit. You know that my dad is a marine, so it's still in the blood that I eat, sleep, and play like one."

Kalie took notice of his decorated office and wondered where he was.

Justin took the hint lightly and peeked over his shoulder at a few of his awards on the bookshelf. "Robbed my mom's trophy case this past summer," he explained. "Had to decorate my own home office with something."

"Understandable."

"I see you have your own."

"Oh, no," she flirtatiously laughed. "I'm at my boyfriend's home for the week."

Almost instantly, Justin's smile dropped. "Did you say—"

"Boyfriend. Yes."

"Oh, wow. I always thought that… umm… nothing. So, what does he do? Where does he study? He's a psych major, too?"

"Pharmaceuticals, actually. He's into… sales. Selling medicine. Trial and error. Tough, really."

"A salesman, Kalie? Seriously? I never pegged you to be a salesman's wife. Do you know that pharms are only paid after the transaction is made? They're always gone, have to have the gift of gab, and they must have distribution. You don't make a sell and bills don't get paid. They make it hard for doctors like me."

"You are so correct on so many levels that it's not even funny."

"Well, it's true. Let's not get on the fact that they take very long business trips."

"You are correct again, Mr. Langston. He's actually on his way back from a trip now."

"How long was he gone this time?"

"Two days. Let's get to the matter of me contacting you a few months ago."

"Ah, yes." Justin took off his Penn State sweatshirt, possibly to showcase his muscular arms that extended from his muscle shirt. "So, I've done some digging for you that I'm pretty sure that you could've Googled. A lot of psych students have started their under the table practices, which is very illegal, yet the pay is very good. The only way to open your own office without getting blacklisted or arrested for illegal practices is to go back to graduate school. There's actually no way around it. I'm sorry to tell you, but your Bachelor's is useless."

"That's depressing."

"Unequivocally."

"*Baby!*"

Kalie barely flinched when she turned away from the monitor. Finding that Scrappy wasn't close as of yet, she decided to salute Justin before there was an even bigger problem. "Hey, umm… thank you." She fingered her locks behind her ear and straightened her specs on her face. "I really appreciate it, Justin. I have to go."

"Are you okay?" He narrowed his lids.

"Yes. I'm fine. My boyfriend just made it in, so you know. We haven't seen each other in a few days."

"Baby!" Scrappy called her again. "You're going to be late to meet your sisters at the mall!"

"Mall trip, huh?" Justin chuckled.

Kalie pursed her lips. "Yes… umm… We're patching up our relationship. You know what? I'm going to message you later. I completely forgot that I was due at the mall."

"Sure. I've missed you, Kay. It was nice seeing you again."

She gave him an awkward smile before lipping, "Bye."

Scrappy stepped into the room as if he was in a hurry, scaring the daylights out of her. "Babe," he called breathlessly.

Kalie turned to him with wide eyes.

"Get up. What are you doing? You're supposed to be there in thirty minutes."

"Hey, babe!" she sang sarcastically. "My day was fine. How was your trip?"

"Don't do that." Scrappy rushed into the room and headed for the closet. Shortly after, he returned with an outfit on a hanger and laid it across the bed. "You're wearing that. Get in the shower. Today is about you and the girls. Go and enjoy yourself."

Kalie rolled her eyes as she stood.

Scrappy had no choice but to paste his eyes on her backside in her black tights. For her to be so athletically fit, her thighs, hips, and ass seemed to have been growing there lately.

"Babe?"

He blinked and found her eyes. "You. Shower. Now."

"But, Scraaap," she whined.

"Baby, I miss you too, alright? Y'all planned these trips just to bond. Aren't you the person who is big on bonding? I told you that I would sit down with my parents, in turn, you told me that you and your sisters would work on your relationship. A deal is a deal. I'll make it up to you when you get back, okay?"

"Fine."

Scrappy pulled her close by her hip to kiss her pouting lips. "I'll tell you all about my trip, I promise. Just don't be late."

"I'm going," she said with a groan.

"You're cute in your glasses, though. You're going to have to keep those on later."

"I will," she blushed as she pulled away from him.

Scrappy kept his eyes on her rolling backside as she walked away heading toward the shower. It wasn't until after she closed the bathroom door that her iMessage app popped up on the screen at Scrappy's right. Wondering what the hell made Kalie's computer come on, he bent at the waist to see the message. He squinted at this guy Justin telling Kalie that he really missed her. Then, he took his eyes to the door as if she was standing there. Fear and insecurity flooded him. *What was she doing while he was away?*

———————

Sheena rummaged through designer t-shirts on a rack. Legend hiding her bank card and cash had her fuming inside. He was determined to make her spend his money. Angrily, she searched the rack to find something for herself, but the only things that clouded her mind was still trying to get Tamara to come back to Miami since it had been two months already, Queenie inviting Dolla to eat at the same table with everyone, and Legend forcing her to spend his money. He had a good slapping coming when she returned.

"Why you look so mad?" Mocha slid up beside her to find something good.

"Because I am," Sheena returned through grinding teeth.

Kalie slid in between the two with a smile. "You have to spend your husband's money, Sheena."

"He's not my husband."

"Might as well be. He's going to text you in a little bit to see if you spent anything."

"Fuck Legend."

"Hey, don't talk about my brother-in-law like that."

"You know what really bugs me?" Sheen whirled around to Kalie to stop searching for a moment. "Do you know that his mama hasn't met me yet? He's asked her on multiple occasions to come and have dinner or breakfast with us, but she chooses to pass it up. What the fuck?"

"Maybe she's not ready."

"Or, maybe she's aware that you're cursed," Mocha offered.

Sheena squinted. "Excuse me?"

Mocha rolled her eyes and turned away from the shirts with a smirk. "You're a Devieux. Queenie's girls are cursed. We're not meant to be happy. If we are happy, then it comes with stipulations."

"Stipulations, huh? Like what?"

She took a deep breath and moved Kalie aside. "I dated a very successful man, whom I helped to skyrocket to another level. He used me. Kalie has certificates and cords of honors. Her first love interest is mental, while the one on the sideline raped her. You—"

"I don't even want you to say anything about rape, Michelle."

"And why not? That's what he did."

"Don't you fuckin' act like you care about anybody getting raped."

"What's that supposed to mean?"

"You mean to tell me that you honestly don't know what I'm talking about?"

"Yes!" Mocha flailed her arms from frustration.

Kalie had no choice but to look between the two to try and figure out what was going on.

"When I was seventeen, Mama took bids on my virginity." Sheena placed her hand on the round hip of her skinny jeans.

"As she did me." Mocha crossed her arms underneath her breast.

"Just after that, we had one of her infamous house parties to fund Kalie's next year of tuition."

"So?"

"You walked in on a john choking the shit out of me, Michelle."

"And?"

"I fucking reached for you. I know that you saw my torn dress and the tears in my eyes."

"What does that have to do with anything?"

"He was *raping* me!" Sheena covered her mouth almost embarrassed by her outburst and at how some of the customers stopped shopping just to stare at her. As soon as Kalie reached for her, she whirled away from her sister's grasp and briskly walked away from the store altogether.

Kalie, with Mocha on her heels, couldn't stop her until she reached Legend's Lexus. "Can you stop for a second?"

"No!" she shouted as she turned on the heels of her sneakers. "This bitch has known for years what happened to me, and she never spoke up about it!"

"I didn't know!" Mocha defended herself.

"Even after I explained to you what you saw, Michelle?"

"I thought that was his thing! He was a customer!"

"He wasn't my fucking customer! You never spoke up about it! You never even asked Mommy why she took me out of the field after that! I had to come up with a fucking excuse because you never supported me or told me that it was okay to open my mouth!"

"If you didn't speak about it, then why should I have?"

Sheena's jaw dropped.

Kalie tilted her head at her oldest sister with squinted eyes. "How the fuck can you say something like that?"

"Well—"

"That's because she's delusional and fucking selfish," Sheena cried.

Kalie had never witnessed her sister crying. She had always thought of Sheena as Superwoman.

"How am I selfish?" Mocha asked her as if the wind had been knocked out of her. "I'm out here, trying to bond with my sisters after all the shit that I've said and done, yet I'm selfish?"

"He was *your* fucking client," Sheena shouted so loud that her veins were popping out of her neck. "If he was supposed to be with you, then what the fuck was he doing with me?"

"I thought that maybe you wanted the cash! Trasheena, I didn't know!"

"You're one fucked up person, and it's fine. I'm over the fact, and I've known how selfish and self-centered you can be."

"If it was me, then it wouldn't have happened."

"Really?" Kalie squealed. "How the fuck can you say something like that while rape victims are standing before you?"

"Because it's true! I would've fought—"

"I fought, but it didn't make any difference! Sheena's right when she says that you're self-centered as fuck because that isn't, in any shape or form, something to say to somebody who's gone through that."

"Fuck this. Y'all bitches want to be emotional, then fine. I just came out to try and have a good time, but this bitch got to bring up an honest mistake from the past, and you just can't stop being a fucking psychiatrist for one second to see that I'm meaning no harm. Fuck you, Sheena, and fuck you, Kalie." Mocha stormed off to find her car, hoping that her sisters wouldn't follow her. Maybe it was the gap in between their years that wouldn't allow them to understand her. Maybe it was the fact that Mocha really didn't understand how to handle the situation. It was still a burden, and they would have to walk through fire together just to get over it.

CHAPTER NINE

House And Home

*C*almly had just sent a text to Mocha to see how she was feeling. It had been a week since she fell ill without telling the others. Some days she didn't want to get out of bed, and some days her skin looked so dry that he wanted to slather baby oil on her. She even had fevers which he had to help fight with ice water and cold packs that he stored in the freezer. She was deathly afraid of going to the doctor, but he didn't know why. She was hiding something. He just didn't know what. He knew that she was sick. He could see it and feel it when he laid next to her. The trouble was convincing her to see someone about it.

"Calm," Legend called him.

He turned away from the doors of the boutique where they had been browsing around for the last hour and a half to see what his Spanish twin could've wanted. He found Legend holding a diamond choker in his hands. Legend was truly inspecting it as if he was the jeweler that they were practically holding hostage.

"Having an emotional Devieux is going to eat us out of house and home," Calmly announced as he shook his head.

Legend sucked his teeth as he gently placed the necklace back on the display of a black velvet bust. "I'm just lucky that Sheena even lets me hold her at night, man. And stop complainin'. We still have to go shoppin.'"

"Why did you have to go to your mama for advice?" Calmly playfully pushed Legend out of the way to take a look inside the display case that he stood in front of. "Getting advice from another woman most definitely costs money, one way or the other."

Scrappy chimed in once he found a ring that he was looking for. "Shut up, Calm. Having a quiet woman is a dangerous thing. Ain't none of them opening up. Ain't none of them giving us a clue as to what they had an argument about. I'm just glad that we ain't done shit to make them walk around the house with puffed up jaws. Now, get over here and tell me if y'all think that Kay would like this. The last thing I want her to do is neglect my proposal."

"You sure you want to do this?" Calmly asked him as he crossed Legend to take the ring out of his old friend's hand.

"Very sure. I got to lock her down or else..."

"Or else?" Legend asked with a cocked brow.

"I feel like she's ready to burn the fuck off. I mean, would you stay after being raped, threatened, and finally shot in the chest? Then, we got Queenie's drama. It's safe to admit that the Devieux women are difficult as fuck to love."

Legend gently took the ring from between Calmly's long nails that he always kept at office-appropriate length and well-manicured. "Teddy *Bro-sevelt*... I don't think that trapping her into marriage will keep her with you. I mean, yeah, it will, but that's not the route you want to take if you're not mentally, emotionally, and financially ready."

"I know I'm ready. I don't want to wake up another damn day without Kay and the assurance that she's going to continue to be there for days to come. That... and I'm already scared shitless that she's going to up and leave."

"Why you scared, though?"

Scrappy ran his hand down his face. "This is gonna sound real insecure when I say this shit out loud... but I guess it was gonna have to be said one way or the other." He then took the ring back, set it on the counter, and pulled his boys away from any other listening ears. "She got an email the other day from a dude asking her if she was going to continue her education the coming semester in the winter. They went on havin' this long ass conversation, takin' a walk down memory lane and shit... and then he tells her that he misses her at his frat parties and how shit just ain't the same. He then goes on to send her a picture of them with him in his frat shirt and her on his back. It made me think of how this dude got shit goin' for himself. He's gettin' a Doctorate in Medicine from Penn State, a part of a frat, and he's one of those athletic motherfuckers. I'm just the connect with a daughter who has pull in Miami. Meanwhile, my girl is a psychologist, got her own practice that's she's opening after furthering her education, and can afford a fuckin' foreign whip on her own. How does that look?"

"Okay, one..." Legend looked over his shoulder and shouted, "Sir, can you gift wrap that ring and fit it in a size...?"

"Five," Scrappy mumbled.

"Five! And can you engrave it with something sweet. Say, something like… Forever, my Kalie. But, can you put in it French or some shit?"

The older gentleman at the counter gave him a simple nod.

"Alright, now, two… Man the fuck up, Scrap. Who gives a fuck about this nigga? He's got all this bullshit and is a colorful motherfucker, okay? You're motherfuckin' Scrap Dawg. Nobody makes a move in Little Haiti or in Miami without consulting you or us. Fuck his frat. You're a Flocka. We got Miami behind us, fool."

Calmly pointed his thumb at Legend. "Other than hyping you up to remind you who you are, you notice that he only sent emails? That means that he ain't got Kalie's number. I bet you that Kay's little square ass only sent him shorter messages than what he was sending her."

"She did," Scrappy lowly admitted.

"See. That's because she's not into him. You think she's gonna leave you and Phara behind for some frat boy when she's got a whole man in front of her? Grab your damn balls, Scrappy. Baby K wasn't even into Bandz's motherfuckin' ass, and he was considered a prince."

"I guess you're right."

"*Know* that I'm right. Now buy this ring and slip it onto her finger when she least expects it, so we can get this over with."

"What he said," Legend agreed. "Now, if y'all will excuse me, I have to go and break my damn bank account and get ready to have my neck broken too when my woman finds out how much money I spent that wasn't hers."

"Wait… what?"

"Oh, Sheena doesn't like for me to spend money on her because she always preaches about having her own money. Told her I was goin' shoppin', and she tried to hand me her bank card. I left that shit under her pillow. If she wanna fight about it, then that's what we're going to do."

"Y'all have the strangest relationship ever."

Scrappy stood there in his thoughts, hoping that his boys were right about Kalie only being for him.

———————

Kalie checked her phone after getting out of the car. It was already ten at night, and she just knew that Scrappy was going to be upset at her for taking on long hours just to earn enough funds to be able to stash money of her own for rainy days. Surprisingly, the text message that she had gotten from him simply stated that he loved her.

A smile stretched upon her face when she saw it as she slid her key inside the lock on her front door. She pressed the phone icon next to his name so that she could call him. It rang on her end, but she could soon hear her ringtone on the other side of the door. Kalie frowned, opening her door to enter into her home.

Scrappy didn't answer, which sent up red flags. She followed the sound of his ringing phone into her bedroom where she found his phone sitting on the edge of her king-sized bed. Surrounding it were rose petals in the shape of a heart. Her smile grew larger. Kalie finally hung up to peel off her shoes. She traveled throughout the home to try and find him, but he wasn't there. She figured that he had gone away to do something else for her. It was either that, or he was very good at playing hide and seek.

She decided that it would've been best to change out of her day clothes to get a little more comfortable, yet as soon as she opened her closet, her chest caved. Scrappy had placed all of her clothes on one side of it, along with a few shopping bags. Kalie waddled inside the closet after losing her breath to run her fingers along his hanging outfits and fitted caps. Her jaw wouldn't snap shut as of yet. She couldn't believe that, while she was at work, he had the energy and time to do all of this.

After swiping away a few stray tears, she had gotten out of her clothes and headed to her master's bath just to make sure that she was clean and fresh by the time her man would come back. Opening the door, she screamed and covered her naked body.

"Yo, you're going to wake Phara with all that noise, girl," Scrappy told her from the tub. "Can't you see that I'm trying to relax? You're fuckin' up my vibes."

Kalie pursed her lips. She couldn't stop her tears. He had drawn a bubble bath inside her hybrid Jacuzzi and was sitting there with all his muscular and tattooed glory before her. For him to move all of his clothes in and to know that Phara was asleep in the room she chose for the girl, meant more than Scrappy could imagine.

"Are you going to stand there and cry, or are you going to come over here and join me?"

Kalie bit her bottom lip as she made the long walk over to her tub to step in. The water was still hot, so she had to stand there for a moment to adjust to the temperature. In standing there, she could see the lust in Scrappy's eyes with all of her womanhood on display. She didn't mind. She knew that he only had eyes for her anyhow.

Scrappy hoped that she wouldn't become offended if she drew over to him because she would feel how erect he was.

Reluctantly, she walked over to him, and then leaned in to kiss his lips. Scrappy couldn't let her leave just yet. He clamped his teeth gently around her bottom lip to send a chill up her spine. She knew what to expect when he had gotten what she called feisty.

When he released her lip, Kalie turned around and slowly sat in the island of bubbles. His rod poked her once she was close enough, but it was a pleasant surprise. Kalie sat anyhow, allowing his member to slide between the cheeks of her backside just to tease him. Relaxing her back against his abs, Scrappy saw the healed bullet wound and kissed it before she could close the space between them. He couldn't help but to feel that it was his fault that she was almost murdered.

Kalie shuttered at the feeling of his lips against her wound. There was no doubt that he was hers and she was his. She loved everything about her Scrappy. His temper, his grimace, his goofiness, his sensitive side that she was trying to become adjusted to, and the love he had for Phara. She relaxed against his hardened frontal and fondly lay her head against his bicep. "This is nice, baby."

Scrappy kissed her neck ever so tenderly that he caused Kalie to squeeze her thighs together. "I figured that you deserve to relax for a minute. But I got to be honest with you."

"About?" she seemingly hummed her question.

"I don't like how you have to stay out past five to get shit done,

Kay. I'm not comfortable with that; especially when thinking of what happened a few months ago. I mean, I know you're packin' now, and I know that you can hold your own, but, baby, it's just on my mind, and I had to get it out."

"Way ahead of you, Scrap. I moved around some appointments today. I'm tired of going through my notes around eight and don't end up done until nearly ten. I thank you for telling me, though. I like how you're opening up to me here lately. I feel special, baby."

"You should." He softly stroked her arm with the edges of his knuckles. "You know that Phara and I will be here a lot more to get her adjusted to it before we move in altogether?"

"Yes." Her smile reappeared. It was so grand that she didn't want it to go away at the thought of having her own little family right there with her.

"I never asked you why you took a shining to my daughter like you did, Kay. I think it's time for you to open up about that. And don't give me no bullshit about how you don't want to right now. Also, we need to go to a grievance counselor."

"For?" She had to look over her shoulder at him in that moment.

"Baby, we didn't know how to take what happened to you; what Bandz did to you. It's like, now you have this strange codependency on me and Phara. I see the way you look when you're coming to meet us, or before you come home. You don't look like you're having a good day until you see us. It's like… nothing is ever right until you have us close. You can pretend all you want, but part of my job is paying attention, baby. I wouldn't be who I am if I didn't notice things."

"Scrappy—"

"You're still having nightmares."

"Baby—"

"We're going, and that's the end of it, Kalie. We both need to know how to get through this, and we're at the point where we can't do it on our own. For you to have studied the mind, you should be aware of this. Very well aware, actually. I'm not going to allow you to break when I can stand in and help." As if to be reading her thoughts, he wrapped his arms around her waist to hold her tight in the tub. Scrappy sensed her body tensing at the thought of how brutally Bandz had taken advantage of her, and like always, he held her to help the thoughts to go away. "What if I'm not there when those images come back to you, Kalie? What if they come back in the middle of you being with a client? And don't think that I don't know that you're taking on more people, not for the money, but to run from the thoughts. You should know that you can't run forever. Don't worry though. I'll be sitting right beside you, babe. Always. You don't ever have to look too far to find me. I wouldn't let you go through anything alone."

"Why are you so good to me?" she screamed with tears waterfalling down her cheeks.

"Because I love you," he whispered, kissing her wet cheeks.

Scrappy rested his forehead against her neck. Yes, he was ready to marry her and to live happily ever after. However, he knew that she wasn't ready and wasn't as close to it as he was. If he proposed on the spot, she would only say yes because she was running.

CHAPTER TEN

Just Not Good Enough

*C*almly couldn't make love to Mocha, she looked horrible. Something was very wrong, and it was more apparent when he heard her scream in the middle of the night. His back shot up off the warm sheets beneath him to find that she wasn't in bed next to him as he had originally thought she was. He jumped out of bed and scurried into the bathroom where she was on the floor with lightly colored fluid in a pool surrounding her. There was no time to waste. He grabbed her off the floor and jogged down the steps to the first floor with her. Through the kitchen he'd gone to get to the garage so that he could place her inside the car as if she was a toddler needing the help. Keeping safety first, he buckled her in, and then closed the door.

He had to go all the way back up to the room to snatch their phones off the chargers, grab her purse, his wallet, and stuff an extra jersey knitted dress inside her handbag in case she needed a change. Almost forgetting a fresh pair of panties for her, he had to B-line for the dresser to retrieve them, finally slipping into a pair of Nikes afterward.

By the time he had got into the car, Mocha was sobbing and

pressing down onto the armrests on either side of her. "What are you doing?" she asked through the pain.

He waited until he threw her purse into the backseat to answer her question. "I'm taking you to the ER."

"No! Baby—"

"Goddammit! You're going! I don't want to hear shit else about it! I should've taken you a week ago!"

"No," she quietly cried. Mocha didn't have any energy to fight with him. In her mind, she was facing the truth finally; that what she had been planning on all this time was being taken. Maybe it was karma. Maybe it was nature.

———

Sheena had just had a bad dream before she was rudely awakened at three in the morning by her boyfriend. They too had to dress quickly. As soon as they stepped off the elevator, there were tears in her eyes when she located Kalie pacing in the waiting room. Just before she could lock her into a hug, they heard their sister's ferocious scream. They both had to jet down the hall to get into the room.

Calmly was coming out when they were going in. His head hung. Tears were in his eyes that he didn't care to wipe away. Legend stood by, waiting for his boy to get close enough. Scrappy grabbed him inside a manly hug to keep him from doing something crazy.

Soon, Calmly's shoulders began to shake. Legend came up to the side of them to wrap his arms around them both. The inevitable had happened, and it cut Calmly way deeper than anyone had expected.

Calmly broke away from them both and punched the wall in front of him. Without feeling his fist throb, he grabbed at his Caesar fade with a look upon his face that every man could identify with when they were torn in two. "It's my fault," he suddenly bellowed. "If I would've taken her to the fuckin' doctor instead of compromising, listening to her tell me that she was alright—"

"Bro, it's not your fault." Scrappy reached for him, yet Calmly whirled away.

"How, Scrap? How the fuck is it not? She told me that it was just a bug! I should've—"

"Where's my daughter?" Queenie asked, barreling down the hall in her slip-ins, pajamas, and bonnet. "Calmly… what's wrong? What happened?" Terror graced her face.

"*I* did this," Calmly admitted with puffy eyes and a red face. No one had ever seen him cry, and at that moment, he didn't care. "I should've followed my first mind. I should've just taken her when I felt that something was wrong!"

Queenie pulled him into a hug, bringing his face into her bosom. "It's alright. Everything will be fine, Calmly. Keep your sanity, young man. You have to hold strong for her, alright. This too will pass, and y'all will have a whole gang of kids, you hear me? Let me get in here to Mocha, but you try to pull yourself together. Be the man that I know you are."

Calmly didn't hear a word she had said. He was busy hating himself. When Queenie released him, he plopped down into a chair with his boys surrounding him. A nurse came out of Mocha's room with something bundled inside covers. Queenie took a deep breath to try and compose herself before facing her oldest.

"It's my fault," Mocha sobbed against Kalie's ribs. Her sister was holding her from the side, stroking her locks ever so tenderly. "I didn't want to face the truth. I didn't want to know. I didn't want this to happen."

Queenie looked down at Sheena on the side of the bed, crouching with her hands in prayer position. She was visibly shaking in her sweat shorts and t-shirt. "My baby," she said to Mocha.

Her eyes wouldn't leave the clear baby bed where the nurse had just taken her stillborn son. She was still in shock at seeing the beautiful little boy all grey and wrinkled but lifeless. She wanted him. He was hers.

"Kalie, what happened?"

Kalie barely turned her wet face to let her mother see the damage of tragedy soaking her cheeks. "It was a boy." Her voice cracked. "Seven pounds, three ounces. His name is Julián Riker Devieux- Cortez."

"Cortez?"

Kalie then took her eyes down to the ring on Mocha's finger. Though it was a promise ring, Mocha had already cried about the promises and dates that Calmly had told her of. "They were going to have a secret wedding next month before Riker arrived. They were going to wed and have him christened under his rightful father's name."

Queenie's heart fluttered when seeing her daughter with her gown hanging halfway off her shoulder and holding both her sisters' hands with either of her own. Her feet were still in the stirrups, and she glistened with sweat. The look of heartbreak was all over her face with how her jaw was hanging slightly ajar, and her natural brows were pressed up into a high V shape.

"Honey," she softly called to Mocha as she rounded the foot of the bed. "I know that this hurts, okay? I do. We can get through this as a family. You have plenty of support around you."

Mocha's head slowly leaned off of Kalie's side. Her hurt eyes met her mother's. Out of all the things she could say to the woman, she chose, "Get out," no higher than a whisper. "Go back to your businesses, *Mommy*. Leave me and my sisters to this."

"Michelle—"

"Get *out!*"

"Go, before she starts hemorrhaging," Sheena told her as she stood. "You came, you showed your face and your support, and that's fine. We got it from here."

"All of you forget that I'm your mother." Queenie was offended.

"No. No, we don't. How could we forget when you want to control every damn thing?"

"This is not about me. My daughter needs me."

"She wants you to leave. That's what she needs you to do."

"All of you are foul. I'm trying to be a mother!"

"For the first time in your damn life. We're not doing this on this day. We lost a baby. The best thing for you to do is what Mocha has told you to do until she's ready."

"Well," Queenie said breathlessly as she backed away from the bed. "I see you're all grown women. Clearly, you'll come to me when you need me."

Sheena's nostrils flexed as she watched her mother leave with what dignity that she had left.

As soon as the door closed, Mocha sucked in a sharp breath that made her sisters think that she was on the verge of having a panic attack. "I love, you Julián," she sobbed. "I love you so much…"

Kalie and Sheena wrapped their arms around her as tight as they could to give her the love that she definitely needed in that moment. Neither of them remembered their argument or even cared about it.

CHAPTER ELEVEN

Sorry Isn't Sweet Enough

*A*t the sound of the alarm, Kalie rolled over to face the alarm clock. As her eyes adjusted, her nostrils flexed to inhale the scent of Perry Ellis. Slowly she sat up in bed to have the covers fall at her lap. Scrappy was standing outside of the closet, staring at himself in the full-body mirror on the back of the door. She rubbed her sleepy eyes when trying to figure out what he was all dressed up for and how come he hadn't gotten her up sooner.

"Baby?" she called him with a raspy voice. "What are you doing?"

Scrappy coyly buttoned the top button of his striped, white, red, and royal blue polo. He realized that he had crawled back inside his shell because he hadn't spoken much since Mocha and Calmly lost Julián. Atop of the fact that Kalie was still corresponding with this Justin character. He had all the pieces to his life but couldn't seem to fit them all together. His boy was hurting, and he felt that he couldn't be there for Calmly the way he needed to. Legend told him of how he and Sheena barely had a good day without faking a smile or two, and Kalie just wouldn't slack up on the work hours as she had promised. She still had yet to tell him about going back to graduate school. Things had shifted over the last month. Nothing was the same.

"Breakfast. With my… womb donor," he told her.

"Did you—"

"I already took Phara to school."

"Babe, her—"

"Lunch was on the island. I know."

"Her extra inhaler—"

"Is in her backpack. I'm her father, Kalie. I know these things."

Kalie gulped as she pulled the covers up to her chest and hugged herself.

"Kay."

She looked up at him with tears swelling in her eyes. The tension in the room was so thick that it made her more than uncomfortable. Like the others, she and Scrappy barely shared a word without throwing on a fake smile. She could only wonder what she had done to make him stop speaking to her the way he used to. Kalie was merely shivering in her place. She didn't like to fear him, but that's where she was when she wasn't in love with him.

"Who is Justin Langston?"

Her eyes grew wider. How the hell could he have known about Justin?

"I don't want to repeat myself, so it's best that you tell me."

"He's… an old friend from Penn State. I mean, I wouldn't call him that now, but he's done some research to make sure that I had to go back to grad school so that I could legally open my own practice."

"Why did you have to go to him when you could've looked it up yourself?"

"Because sometimes, results are misleading. I don't really have contact with any of the people who I graduated with who also study psychology. He's told me that they make under the table money as well, but I don't want to do that for the rest of my life, you know? I got my answers, so I don't speak to him anymore."

Scrappy left it at that. He knew for a fact that she didn't speak to him because, in the last few weeks, he had a routine of waiting until she fell asleep to check her phone for this character. He would snoop through her social media accounts, emails, texts, and other apps where this Justin could've tried to get in contact with her.

"Did you have feelings for him?" he asked honestly.

"God, no!" Kalie shouted with a look of disgust. "Scrappy, Justin was so full of himself and valued his status in his frat, among what he called his epic frat parties, more than he valued his grades or life itself. I just used him because I knew that he had a wide network of people that he could go to for the answers I needed. Justin is a slime-ball who is destined to marry a stuck up broad who just wants to be on the arm of a black doctor. Don't insult my integrity like that again. I have standards, you know. Hence the reason that I'm with you."

"Why are you here with me instead of someone who's educated and born into money?"

"Where the fuck else am I supposed to be, Edwin?" she asked

angrily. Her brows squeezed tightly together before she had the realization that Scrappy was insecure. Her features softened as her lips formed a small 'O'. "Baby… you think… you… Justin?" Kalie pulled the covers and swung her feet over the edge of the bed. "Scrappy, I love you. Why wouldn't I be with you? I love your complexity, your vigilance, your strength, your mental capacity, your heart, your views… Why the hell would I be into anything less?"

"Do you really think you need to be here instead of there?"

"Yes!"

"Why?"

"Because of you and Phara! Justin can't feed my mind, my soul, or my heart like you and Phara! Who the fuck are you to question our love, Edwin Broadus? I've been here through you breaking down, going to jail, possibly losing your daughter, her possibly dying, me possibly dying, and you want to stand there and question me over a guy who can roll over and die and I wouldn't give a fuck about it?"

"Baby—"

Kalie threw her hand and traveled into the bathroom, slamming the door behind her. Her heavy bladder threatened to be released. She pulled her sleeping shorts and panties down to have a morning pee, only, the date dawned on her. She looked down into the seat of her panties, finding them clean still. With a hardened face, her tears finally fell. Scrappy was going to be a father again, yet she didn't know how or when to tell him since it appeared that he was questioning their relationship.

Mocha pulled her head out of the toilet for the second time in three hours. She couldn't understand what was happening to her body. All she knew was that the heavy-duty antibiotics that the doctors had her on made her feel like shit.

Calmly entered the bathroom in only his black briefs to wet a towel and handed it to her. Afterward, he was out of there and inside his closet. He had work to do after the guys had already returned from Jacksonville. He had gone back to being a drone. He counted, weighed, stacked, checked on his boys, and clocked three to four hours of a sleep after cruising through Little Havana to make sure that his people were okay. After falling in love and having something solid snatched away from him, he feared that that's what his life was only meant to be again— work and a cat nap.

Mocha sniffled as she waddled out of the bathroom. She was only lucky that she had been released from the hospital two weeks prior to the date after being what she called a prisoner until they were able to remove as much infection as possible.

She cleared her throat before speaking. "There's a club that's for sale on Collins," she weakly told him as she made her way to the closet for her purse and keys. "I think you should look into turning that into a strip joint. You can even run your girls in and out of there. I remember that you bought some the last quarter that Dolla had a showcase. It's just an idea to stack revenue."

Calmly closely watched her as she slipped inside her loafers and grabbed her handbag off the floor. "What the fuck are you doing?"

"Oh, and if you open a strip club, you can make a killing on your ecstasy, weed, and powder."

"Mocha—"

"Only invite Miami's elite to the opening, boost liquor prices and entrance fees—"

"Mo, stop."

She left the closet and walked out of the room while still gabbing on as if she didn't hear him.

"Graphics shouldn't cost you that much, but it's the staff you're going to have to worry about."

Calmly chased after her until he was on the stairs, where he grabbed her by the arm and whirled her around to face him.

Mocha lost her breath. In that instant, staring into his eyes, tears gathered within her own.

He could feel her body vibrating inside his single palm. He knew that she wasn't okay; especially considering the fact that, in a full month, they hadn't held a conversation. "Baby, where are you going?" he asked her with a soft voice.

"Home." Her voice cracked.

"This *is* your home."

"I have a whole condo—"

"That you sold, remember?" He searched through her hollow eyes, hoping that she hadn't lost her mind or slipped away from reality. "The realtor gave you one-point-five million for it. You had me go to the bank while you were in the hospital to deposit his check."

Mocha's bottom lip quivered. She hadn't forgotten that large amount of money. What she did forget was where her home was.

Calmly chose not to say anything further. He wrapped his long and strong arms around her tightly to hold her and make her feel a sense of security. He knew that she was lost. She was all turned around in life and in love. Losing the baby took more of her than either of them could've imagined.

Mocha pulled away from him as tears streamed down her cheeks. She fished her phone out of her purse and clicked on her contacts.

"What are you doing now, Michelle?"

She sniffled. "My little sister is supposed to be a bad little motherfucker. I saw her reviews on her Facebook page. She's going to have to put her magic to work. I can't lose me, Carlito. I already lost a part of me. I can't lose anymore."

"You're calling Kalie? Don't you think that's a conflict of interest?"

"Hell naw. Her little ass has some problems of her own that she needs to get through. We might as well get through them together."

Calmly grabbed her phone and gently took it away from her hand.

She looked up at him with red eyes, searching for some kind of approval, and wondered what she could've been doing wrong this time.

"If you do this, you need to remember not to hold anything back. Now, I love you, Michelle, but we can do this together. The both of us."

"You need to be looking into that club—"

"My priority is you. You can't change that, and you can't tell me what to put above you. Like I said, if you're going to do this—"

"I got this. I'm going to have to cut myself open and show her every damn thing because I can't put a wedge between us; even though I feel like there has been one."

"There has been, but consider it gone. I'm here for you. You need to remember that. This is the first full conversation that we've had in a long while, and I don't like that shit. So, you go and meet up with Kay while I go work, and then I'll look into the club. Afterward, we're having dinner. Together. Then, we're going to make love, and you will remember who loves you through it all— loss, bullshit, drama, and everything in between. Don't you ever shut me out again. You got that?"

Mocha hung her head as she coiled her arms around his neck. Gently, she pushed her cheek against his chest to let her tears flow. She could feel the true love pouring out of the tattooed menace. There was no questioning it. She simply overlooked it after losing her first born son. Going to Kalie would be the best decision for them all.

"I'm sorry that we lost our son, babe," he whispered to her. "We can't replace him, but we'll give him a memorial, alright? We'll still cherish him. But we both have to set him free and let him rest in peace."

"It's my fault, baby," she breathlessly admitted.

"No. No, it's not. It's not either of our fault. I need you to stop beating yourself up over this. I've had to stop kicking my own ass, too."

"Did you think it was my fault?"

"No. I never blamed you. I blamed me for not taking you to see someone."

"Then why didn't you talk to me, Carlito?"

"Because you weren't talking to me. I thought that you needed space. I didn't know what to say, if anything. I was just going through the motion. That stops now. You hear me? We had a son together who had to go back to heaven. You have a man who's going to be your husband soon and who won't let you fall into a dark place. Other than that, you have a sister who is specially trained in these sorts of situations and who is, according to her Facebook business reviews, the go-to person for healing. You're a winner, baby. You may have lost something so precious, but it's time to adjust your crown and do what needs to be done."

Mocha looked up into his soulless colored eyes and found the truth. "You adjust yours, too, my king."

To seal their promise, their lips came together. So sweet and so tender, they embraced one another as their first step to healing.

CHAPTER TWELVE

Now Or Never

Kalie was wrapping up an emergency client when her front door came open. Through it stepped the last person she had hoped to see. Kalie gave her client a hug and escorted them to their car before reentering and slamming the door.

"Why are you inside my home?" she angrily asked Queenie. "If I didn't return your calls, what made you think that you were invited here?"

"I missed my daughter," Queenie confessed. "How else am I supposed to get in touch with you?"

"I'm not happy with you and neither are my sisters. I don't want you here."

"Then, I'll pay you to listen to me. That's what you do all day, every day, isn't it?"

"Pardon me, Madam Queenie, for earning a dishonest income without you. Would you like to squeeze out ten percent of my earnings?"

"Don't you mock me, girl."

"Speaking of mockeries. How dare you bring Dolla into the house you built for us, as it's said, knowing that he stabbed everybody there in the back? Money isn't everything, Mommy. It's damn sure not worth losing your kids."

"It's not, but I was trying to explain to you girls that I have the squeeze on him. He's incapable of ever hurting any of you with my leash around his neck, and that includes his brother... whenever I find him."

"Oh?" Kalie giggled as she approached her mother, who was dressed in a simple pair of jeans, a white blouse, and pumps. "The almighty queen of Miami still hasn't found one man?"

"You don't understand how business works."

"Just like you don't understand how motherhood works."

"What did you say to me?" Queenie narrowed her eyes as she took a step closer to her daughter. "You remember who you're talking to."

"I'm talking to a woman who would rather control her daughters than to have their best interest at heart."

"How do you figure?"

"You let Mocha date your enemy, Mama. Prime example. You kept me away out of pure fear that someone's wife would come after me. You let Sheena go so long without real love that it's almost killing her inside her relationship with Legend. She gets very angry at him when he wants her to spend his money or drive his car. Instead of teach us, you've scarred us. Lastly, you invited a snake into your home when you know damn well what that man is capable of. There's a fine line between being a mother and being absolutely overbearing. You slapped me when you thought that I was pregnant by Bandz. Hearing that he raped me, you've done nothing about it like a mother should. There's no need in wondering why we want nothing to do with you."

Kalie went to the door to open it for her mother to leave. She couldn't stand to look at the woman.

"Then that means you have life all figured out." Queenie rubbed her hands together with her head bowed. To her, her daughters just didn't understand how difficult it was to maintain a steady business while watching her back and keeping her other girls safe from harm, and then try to be a mother on top of it all. Dolla's words came back to her of how they'll always be a hybrid. They would be forever split down the middle between the royal side and human beings.

Kalie's front door opened, almost hitting her elbow in the event. Shocked, her head whirled around to see her older, fabulous sister there to visit as she had hoped. However, Mocha wasn't so fabulous. Her hair was combed in waves to the back. She hadn't gone to get her platinum blond extensions as of yet. Her large shades were pulled slowly away from her puffy eyes to show the other two the damage of her spilling more unexpected tears during her drive. Mocha was dressed in a clinging undershirt and black tights that showcased her figure. Kalie could feel the anger vibrating off her sister, so she casually closed the door behind Mocha, and then stood away from the pair in case there were to be swinging fists in the air.

Mocha stared Queenie down. To Kalie, it was old school versus new school. Their hair was the same color and length, yet in different styles. Their figures were the same with one being more taut and paid for while the other was natural and sagging just a tad. Mocha's feet were clad in her black, leather Timberlands, so she was ready to throw down if her mother wouldn't listen to what she had to say. Standing only four inches shorter than the queen, thanks to Queenie's heels, Mocha threw her purse to the ground and took three long and hard steps over to her mother.

Queenie's heart pounded. She didn't want to smack her daughter, but she feared that she was going to have to if Mocha jumped stupid.

Suddenly, Mocha's arms flung forward and wrapped around Queenie's neck. Her face was so numb that she didn't even feel the tears as they fell this time.

Queenie shut her eyes tight, afraid to even breathe.

"Grandma didn't know any better," Mocha breathlessly whispered over her mother's shoulder. "She cursed you, Mommy. In the same case, you returned it without knowing. It's not your fault. It is *not* your fault. Thank you for being better than her. Thank you for not following behind a man. Thank you for teaching us how to be strong. Thank you for teaching us how to watch our shit while being away. Thank you for teaching us how to think and maneuver around situations. Thank you for showing us that when there is no way that it is okay to make one. Thank you for loving us."

Queenie never wanted to show weakness, but she allowed herself to be vulnerable for the sake of her daughters. Her tears spilled over at hearing and accepting Mocha's words. That's all she ever wanted to hear from a young age; that she had done something good.

"I need to get Sheena out here," Kalie said with a shaky voice as she pulled her phone from her pocket. "If it's healing we need, then it's healing we'll get."

———————

Scrappy was wrapping up his work with Calmly and Legend when he received a phone call that he never thought that he would get. Shay had stolen his number out of Tamara's phone while she showered. She had finally had the nerve to show up after so many months. Whatever situation she was in, it must've been a bad one to finally reach out to her sister-in-law for help. Shay told Scrappy that Tamara needed money, so she had hoped that Shay had some of Bartholomew's supposed life insurance money left.

With hatred pumping through his veins, he pulled up behind his ex-brother in law's house with Legend and Calmly getting out of his car after him. The other two went around the house while Scrappy approached the backdoor. Calmly went to the side door, and Legend went around to the front. Tamara couldn't run away this time. She had no choice but to face punishment.

Scrappy turned the doorknob as if it was his home and walked right into the kitchen. Tamara was coming around the corner with a plate in her hand when she froze seeing him there.

"Got somethin' you want to say to me?" he asked her.

She dropped the plate and headed to the front door. As soon as she drew it open, Legend caught her by the throat and pushed her to the ground.

"I don't like hittin' women," Legend told her angrily. "If I were you, I wouldn't hit me back, bitch."

With fear flooding her chocolate face, she scooted back on her ass.

"You've been duckin' me after you tried to kill my daughter and my girl." Scrappy grabbed her by the hair to pick up from the floor. "Get your ass in the trunk. You got somebody else to see."

"Yo, Scrap!" Legend called while Scrappy was hustling with fighting Tamara to get her to the backdoor. "At least we didn't break nothin' this time!"

Scrappy pushed her out of the backdoor.

Tamara figured that, since he released her, then she could try to make a run for it. Wrong idea. As soon as she hit the corner, Calmly shoved her back down to the ground.

"Where you goin'?" he asked her, snapping the top of his gun. "This bitch turned into a track star. The same bitch that almost killed my niece. You can either get the fuck up or have me explaining to my wife why I killed a bitch today."

Tamara gulped as she slowly rose to her feet. She gasped when she turned because she was staring right inside of Scrappy's blue eyes that were filled with rage. "I'll go," she surrendered with her voice quivering.

Legend waved his hands in the air. "Get yo' bitch ass in the trunk so we can get this over with. You ain't gon' be not another damn issue for my bro."

Tamara couldn't break her connection with Scrappy. Neither could she cry. He was the same man that she was sure she could break and turn her into something more soft. To no avail. She was looking right into the eyes of the monster that she helped to create. Being cornered, she had no choice but to cooperate with the demands all around.

Successfully, Legend closed the trunk after Tamara crawled in and had placed a strip of duct tape around her wrist and over her mouth. Afterward, he got in the backseat, concealing his piece in the pocket of the driver's seat. "That's one issue solved," he said as Scrappy started his car. "What about Bandz and Dolla? When can we get rid of these fuckin' fools?"

Calmly smacked his teeth. "They're Queenie's problem now. I'm not stressin' my baby girl after what we've already been through. Whenever she's okay and she gives me the okay to do somethin' about him, then I'll let y'all know."

"Scrap?"

"You heard him," Scrappy responded. "One problem at a time, my brotha. One problem at a time. Consider them blessed as fuck by Mocha." Finally, he pulled out of the slim driveway to head to his home. He was going to present Tamara to Kalie and wait for her to tell him what to do because the last thing he needed to do was upset her about the slightest thing.

CHAPTER THIRTEEN

Confessions

With confessions all around and a deeper understanding of their mother's childhood, the women felt lighter than a feather. They understood that she was overprotective, with it coming off as controlling, because she didn't want anyone taking advantage of her girls the way it had been done to her. Everyone spilled their apologies and shared memories of their childhood. The afternoon was a very beautiful one until the mention of Dolla was put out on the table. Queenie admitted that it wasn't just for the money that she allowed Dolla to come back. She told them of how she wanted to make him weak and vulnerable until Mocha snapped back from the baby so that she could do the honors of finishing him off for all he'd done.

Kalie gave her sisters hugs after they helped her pack another week's worth of clothes so that she could spend it with Phara and Scrappy. Queenie, of course, sat on her daughter's bed with a glass of wine in her hand.

Mocha came out of the closet with a corset dangling on the edge of her finger; her head was tilted to the side at the sight of it. "And what the fuck is this for?" she asked Kalie. "Your ass ain't a buck-fifty, soaking wet. The hell you need a corset for?"

Kalie left her chest of drawers to snatch it away from her sister. "It's just for the bedroom," she playfully, yet shamefully, admitted.

"Y'all so nasty!"

"Speaking of nasty and being skinny," Sheena commented as she rose from the floor and adjusted her baseball cap over her eyes. "Her ass is going to need that corset with the way she's gaining weight. Look at them thighs and ass. Just growin'. The girl only eats once a day and runs eight miles like she's a marine or somethin'. She even has a little belly now."

The room grew quiet as they all had a shocking realization that Kalie just couldn't hide anymore.

Queenie swirled her wine around in her glass as she leaned back. "So, Baby K… When are we due?"

"I'm not sure," she quietly responded.

Mocha's jaw dropped. "Why didn't you say something?" she screamed.

She turned to her sister with a hanging head. "I thought that I would've spoken up the day at the mall, but we had a falling out. Then, you lost our nephew… so it would've been inappropriate. Other than that… I remember you being insanely jealous of me, so I didn't want you to think that I was trying to steal some sort of shine from you."

"Bullshit, Kay! This is a whole baby!" Mocha marched over to her sister and threw her arms around her shoulders. When she pulled back, she looked over her shoulder at Sheena. "You want to tell us that you're pregnant, too? We can have ghetto twins!"

"Bitch, no." Sheena rolled her eyes. "Birth control and condoms. Legend is not getting a little mutt out of me until I get a ring. I love him, but I'm not about to be girlfriend forever, or girlfriend turned baby mama. Not happening."

"You so damn hard! Give that ass up and spit out a couple babies."

"Hell naw. He can have the ass, but no babies. Speaking of which, I need to be gettin' out of here to get dinner started. I don't need his mama sayin' something else about me. That old witch can't stand my ass."

"It's not that she can't stand you," Queenie spoke up. "She just thinks that her son can do better. I'm not saying that to be mean because my baby is the best fuckin' candidate to be his wife. I'm saying it because I know that that's how mothers think of their kids. Now, I couldn't stand Dolla, and yes, I wanted Mocha to do her job. But when she fell in love with him, instantly I knew that she could do better. I'm a mother. I wanted her to have better. Calmly? He is better on every single level. Maybe he doesn't make the money that Dolla made, but I know that he's passionate and that he wouldn't hurt my baby. He ain't sneaky, he ain't fake, and he ain't a slitherin' damn snake who sucks the life out of my daughter because he can't do better for himself. By the way..." Queenie looked to Mocha then as she sipped from her glass. "When is he giving you that wedding?"

Mocha scoffed. "When everything settles down. He doesn't want me to stress at all, and I'm good with that."

"Cool. My doll, Ashley, graduates this year, and I want her to make your dress. The girl is bad. If that's not what you want, then that's fine. It's just a suggestion. I know that somebody needs to get married so I can boo-hoo at a damn wedding. These men that y'all have are everything that I wish your fathers were. Sheena's was prince charming with a smile that made me hop up out of my panties. His issue was that I wouldn't quit the business and become his submissive housewife. The only problem with that, when I look back on it, was the fact that we could've compromised. Since we couldn't, I killed his ass."

All the girls frowned while Queenie took back the last of her drink.

"I'm just playin'," she admitted.

"Ma… we just started all this healing shit," Sheena told her with a straight face. "Don't do that."

"I didn't kill him, but I damn sure made his life a living hell. After he found out I was pregnant with you, all my hopes were up until he backhanded me one good time for me being out all night with a client. I put his ass out, had somebody jump the little bitch he had been cheating on me with, and I hit him with my car."

"Mama!"

"Oh, no, that part isn't a joke. He tried to press charges, so I drained his bank account and set fire to his house."

"Mom!" Kalie squealed.

"That's what he got. But you girls are nothing like me, and I appreciate that about you."

Sheena squeezed her temple. "I shouldn't even ask this question, but where is my dad now?"

"Oh, that little bitch he cheated on me with found out that he was cheating on her. Shot him in the chest multiple times and killed the other bitch, too. I visited her in prison after I had you, just to see if you had any siblings that needed to be taken care of. There are none, fortunately. But there's not a day that goes by that I don't feel sorry for her."

"And why is that?"

"She thought that she was getting something great. Like if she stole him away from me that she would be complete. All she did was take the hell away from me that she had gotten."

"I remember him, Mommy," Mocha said. "I remember the arguments. I remember seeing y'all threatening to fight each other. I never wanted to go through that."

"I'm sorry you saw all of that, but I wouldn't keep a man around like that. I didn't want y'all growing up to think that it was acceptable. I would slit my own wrists open before I let you girls feel weak, helpless, and walked all over. Ain't no way. And what I love about you, Michelle, is the fact that you at least tried with Dolla. You had something to bring to the table to make something with him. When you were done, though, you were done."

"I would love to stand here and continue with all the love," Kalie laughed, "but I do have a man and daughter to get to."

"Nope," Sheena told her with her phone in her hand. "According to this message that Baby just sent me, we're having Phara tonight." She looked up at her sister with a cocked brow. "You told Scrap that you're pregnant?"

"Not yet," she mumbled. "I guess since we're having alone time, I can tell him."

"You do that. I need to head to Little Havana. I don't want a hungry man, a complaining mother-in-law, or a starving niece."

"Remember to use food coloring with red food."

"Kalie, damn, I know. It ain't hard to remember. She doesn't like red food. Shut up."

"Hey!" Mocha called Kalie while her sister was dragging her luggage off the bed. "Do you think me and Calmly can watch Phara tomorrow; just to give Sheena and Legend a break?"

"You don't think it'll be too much?" Kalie responded with a frown.

"No, not at all. I've been dying to keep her as is. Legend and his bitch like to hog babies."

"Don't hate the playa," Sheena told her. She thumped Mocha as she passed. "You need to hate the parents. Fuck outta here."

"Mommy, you comin' home with me?" Mocha asked Queenie.

Queenie rose from the bed, inspecting her empty glass. "If you have wine, I'm all in that thing."

"Bye, Baby K!" Mocha gave Kalie one more hug before leaving. "Yes, you are the shit with this psychiatry business. You need to go on back to grad school so we can fill up your office. Don't forget to put me on the calendar for next week, too."

"I got you," she giggled. "Y'all, turn some of those lights off on your way out!"

"I ain't a maid!" Mocha shouted as she exited. "You better turn your own damn lights off."

With a smile, Kalie shook her head. It was a pleasure to have such a happy family, yet it was about to be snatched away one more time.

CHAPTER FOURTEEN

Damned If You Don't

Scrappy was nice enough to give Tamara a plastic cup of water. She sat on the floor beside the couch, shivering. Since being told that Kalie would decide her fate, she had no idea what the young girl was about to do to her. She didn't know Kalie as a person. She only knew what she saw on Instagram, figuring that the girl was soft. A little too soft to be with someone like Scrappy.

On the loveseat, Scrappy sat with his back against the arm and his Nike clad foot upon the cushion. He cleaned his short nails with a hunter's knife while waiting for his love to arrive. He was just ready to get everything over with; having a mind that after Tamara was out of the way, then everything would be fine.

"Do you remember our walks through Little Haiti?" Tamara asked, no higher than a whisper. "You used to stop and get me shaved ice—"

"Shut up," he returned quietly. "You should've been thinking about all the good shit before you turned stupid."

"I'm sorry—"

"It's too late for your sorry."

The front gate opened with a loud squeal, which made Scrappy jump to his feet. Little did Kalie know, he was always excited for her to come home to him. Of course, she would never see it, but he always was. He took a deep breath and traveled over to the front door. As soon as Kalie stepped through, he caught her in his arms. She felt a little more heavy than she usually was, but he admired the weight gain. It filled her body out in all the right places.

Kalie giggled. "Babe! Why didn't you answer the phone so that you could come and get my luggage out of the trunk? I don't want to hear your mouth about..." She shut off her sentence when seeing something move just out of her line of sight. Kalie turned her head slightly to see Tamara there with a look of sadness and disgust all over her face. "Hello."

Tamara rolled her eyes.

"That's what I get after you tried to kill me?" Kalie pushed Scrappy out of the way, simultaneously dropping the handle of her rolling luggage. "Why are you in my living room?"

"This is my baby daddy's house," Tamara answered smartly. "I was stuffed in a fucking trunk and brought here. Don't act like I asked to be here."

Scrappy closed the gate, locked it, and then closed the front door. "You ain't in no position to talk shit," he told Phara's mother.

Kalie held her hand up as she glided into the living room, stopping shy of where the woman was sitting. "You have no idea how badly my husband, sister, and brother-in-law wanted to kill you, do you? So, if I were you, I would be thankful that it's a hippie and not a gangster that decides your fate. You know, it's baby mamas like you who make it real difficult for the next woman to actually love their men. He does what he needs to do for his daughter, but you just had to make it difficult because he didn't want to be with you."

"Well," Tamara chuckled, "I'm not his and neither is Phara."

Kalie's chin lifted into the air as she slowly backed away.

"What you say?" Scrappy slowly turned to Tamara with his brows squeezing tightly. "You better fuckin' answer me. What did you just say?"

Tamara gulped. "I said... I said—"

Scrappy pushed Kalie out of the way, having her to flop sideways onto the couch, and grabbed the neckline of Tamara's t-shirt. He lifted her just a little off her bottom.

She grabbed his wrists with pure terror pouring out of her eyes. She knew how bad Scrappy could be, but she never thought that he would be that way in front of his precious Kalie.

"Answer me, bitch! Whose is she then?" Scrappy shouted in her face.

"B-B-Bandz's kid," she confessed, thinking that it would get him off her ass and onto Bandz's.

Scrappy dropped her and turned away, sliding his hand down his mouth to compose himself. So many thoughts shot through his mind at once that, had anyone saw the visuals, they would be utterly confused at how he could jump from the first dap he had ever given Bandz, to Phara's birth, and the many scenarios he walked through about killing Tamara and letting her live. Upon reaching a conclusion that he could live with, Scrappy drew his pistol from behind his back and spun around on his heels.

Kalie leaped off the couch and shielded Tamara with her body.

Had Scrappy pulled the trigger, he could've shot the love of his life. For some reason, and fortunately for Kalie, he had hesitated, which was something he rarely had done when in the field.

"Move," he demanded through grinding teeth. "Kalie... move the fuck out of the way. I'm not fuckin' with you. Get on."

Kalie vigorously shook her head with tears streaming down her cheeks at the realization that she could've been a dead woman had her love not gave it a second thought to letting off a stray bullet that had his ex's name on it.

"Move!" he roared.

"No!" Kalie screamed back. "Baby, she's lying. She was just trying to get a rouse out of you. Can't you see that? She just wanted you to end all of her own pain and torment. She wanted you in prison so that she could have Phara back. You were close to that had I not stood in the way. Scrappy, baby, think."

"I'm not stupid!"

"I didn't say that," she told him a little softer as she gathered her nerves to put on a stronger front for him. "Not by a longshot are you stupid. I'm just saying that killing her would be a mistake."

"Kalie, get the fuck out of the way or else I will move you myself."

"Baby—"

With his free hand, he snatched Kalie by her blouse and flung her over to the loveseat. Before she could bounce back, she heard a gunshot and Tamara's scream. Kalie hustled to her feet, shivering. The only thing that she could see was Scrappy standing with his feet at shoulder's length, and his free hand dangling at his side. Tamara slowly fell over onto the floor with her face contorted.

After a moment, she finally let out a wail that shook the walls of the house. "You shot me!"

"Same fuckin' place where you shot my woman," he told her. "Wound for a wound, bitch." With that, he tore away from the living room and traveled into his bedroom where he slammed the door behind him.

Kalie swallowed her fear and stood tall. "Get up," she told Tamara. "Stand the fuck up!"

Tamara, with glistening cheeks, struggled to her feet while holding the hole in her chest near the joint of arm and collarbone.

"You brought this on yourself," Kalie explained. "You're lucky that he didn't just end it all. Now you go live with the fact that you helped to destroy a man. Whether he is Phara's father or not, you have to live with the fact that he still has full custody, and now she has a new mother. You live with the fact that you were stupid and almost murdered the woman who spared your fucking life. Get out of our house and you stay far away. If not, there will be no mercy the next time. And, oh, if someone asks how you were shot, tell them it was a robbery gone wrong."

Tamara circled Kalie with her eyes hard on her and backed away toward the door. She didn't know how the hell she would get help with this one. It was clear that she needed to stay away from Bandz because she knew that, after her confession, Bandz would be next on the hit list. She wasn't getting caught in the crossfires of that.

Wisely, Kalie locked the gate and front door, and then went to the kitchen to fetch bleach and a sponge. She couldn't risk Scrappy going away when she had so much left to experience with him. Trying to push the craziness and tragedies to the back of her mind, Kalie got down on hands and knees to scrub the hardwood floor near the couch to get Tamara's blood up from it. Then, she had to treat the couch, which would be entirely difficult because the couch was black and leather.

Scrappy could smell the bleach in the air over his lit blunt and frowned. He put it out in the ashtray and rose from the bed, hoping that Kalie wasn't straining herself. Down the hall and into the living room he had gone to find her on her knees with the bucket of hot water at her side. He opted not to ask what she was doing. He already knew. He just didn't think that she would've been the kind to clean up his messes. He considered himself fortunate to have her here instead of in Philadelphia with Justin, where he was sure Kalie would fall in love and marry a good guy, and then pop out a gang of kids without a worry in the world.

"Tie up your loose ends," she suddenly told him with a sniffle. "Do whatever it is you have to do to make sure she stays quiet so that you don't go to prison."

"Baby—"

"We're having a baby, Scrappy. Me and Phara need you more than ever."

Scrappy grabbed her wrist, pulling her off the floor so that she could look at him. "We're what?"

"I mean, I'm not sure how far along I am, and I'm not sure what it is just yet, but I put it around two and half months. Twelve weeks tops."

"Kalie—"

"It's more than important that we're careful with what we do, Scrappy. Not just for us but for Phara and the new baby. Whatever fire we have to walk through, we need to do that shit now to keep our family together and unbothered. We can't risk anything right now. On top of that, I'm going to have to go back to school to finish. But I'm not going to Philly. I've chosen FAU, and it's the closest that I could get to. I'm not leaving you guys behind, and I don't want to take Phara out of her element. Scrappy, I need you to step up and do whatever it is that bad guys do in certain situations to make the impossible possible. Can you do that?"

"Yes," he promised.

"I'm holding you to that." Her hands gently grazed his cheeks to pull his face closer. "No fear. No worry. Just me, you and our kids. If I don't want anything else in this world, Edwin, it's that. Our family. Our happiness."

Scrappy was at a loss of words. There was nothing that he could return. Instead of trying, he sealed their lips for a kiss. In the back of his mind, he was going to have to make sure that Tamara's situation would be settled before he took another step forward to ensure that she wouldn't be poking around. Regardless of who lent their semen to create his prize for a daughter, he was her only father, and he was content in that.

CHAPTER FIFTEEN

Damned If You Do

The very next day, Scrappy put his ear to the ground to catch up to Tamara. She had been admitted into the hospital and was being treated for her bullet wound. He stepped off the elevator all by himself with a single duffle strapped across his chest. With his wrist watch and bracelets gleaming at either side of his heavily starched black shorts, he looked more like he was at the hospital for a business transaction than that of a visit to an injured patient.

As soon as he turned the corner, he found Tamara propped up on her bed channel surfing. She whipped her head around, wondering what the hell he was doing at her room in the first place. Scrappy inched into the room after shoving his hands inside his pockets. Out of his pocket, he pulled his cell phone and sent a text message.

"I came to pay my respects," he said no higher than a whisper. "I just wanted to come up here to tell you thank you for baring down and bringing a life into this world that I absolutely cherish. Had it not been for the daughter you blessed me with, I wouldn't have been smarter. I wouldn't know what real love is. I wouldn't know what it's like to be a dedicated father. So, I thank you. In sparing your life..." Scrappy took the strap from over his shoulder and placed the duffle beside her on the bed. "I'm giving you a hundred and fifty grand to get the fuck away from here after you're healed. It's from me, Legend, and Calmly. When shit hits the fan, myself and wife want you nowhere near it. Even if Phara was fathered by Bandz, I don't give a fuck. She's my daughter, and I'm gonna leave it at that. However, I'm learning from my parents' mistakes, so let me say this. Neither of us were dealt a fair hand growing up. I'm sorry for puttin' my hands on you after all the shit you've done. I'm sorry for neglecting you after our breakup instead of check up on the mother of my kid. I'm most definitely sorry for putting you through whatever hell you faced with me. Things are different now. I'm happy, I'm in love, and I know that that's what you wanted from me, but we have too much poison here for us to remotely make something happen."

"She got you talkin' with some sense," Tamara commented. "Where's your uniform, monkey? She got you on a leash, too?"

Scrappy smiled inside, knowing that it was just her trying to get up under his skin.

"I won't do to Phara what was done to either of us. Your father walked away from your family, and my mother walked away from mine. Neither of them gave us a proper goodbye."

Pattering feet came down the hall until both sets turned the corner. Sheena had Phara by the shoulders to make sure that Tamara wouldn't try anything stupid. Tears welled in Tamara's eyes. This was officially goodbye to her own child.

Tamara held her free arm out for Phara to come to her, being that her other arm was in a sling.

Phara turned her face away and hugged Sheena's leg.

"C'mere, baby," Tamara lowly said with a sniffle.

"She's shy and stubborn," Sheena commented. "Just like her mama and aunts. It's difficult to be a Devieux-Broadus. I assure you."

Tamara squinted and tilted her head at the shade Sheena threw.

Scrappy picked Phara up off her feet and took her over to Tamara's bed. When she turned her head, her single braids and beads covered her faces as such a veil would; just like Scrappy's when he was close to exploding.

Tamara reached for her daughter, but Phara hugged Scrappy's neck so tight that he could hardly breathe.

"I love you," Tamara told her with a quivering voice. "Phara… Mommy loves you."

Scrappy bounced her a little to get her to turn around, but she wasn't budging. "Je veux Kalie, Papa." She told him that she wanted Kalie.

Of course, Tamara could understand her with her second language being French. It squeezed her heart to know that her own daughter wanted nothing to do with her. It hurt more than Scrappy leaving.

"Goodbye, Tamara," he told her. Then, he backed away from the bed to leave her alone, which was how she made it after all she had done.

It wasn't so easy for him to turn away one last time, but he knew that he had to for the sake of his livelihood and his daughter.

Sheena stared Tamara down as the young woman cried silently, hating the fact that she wasn't able to get her hands on her before Scrappy sent her away.

A week had gone by with the gang patching up their broken relationships and cracked lives. The guys made sure that the girls were actually able to have fun after a while of being pent up and sad. They had gone to Jacksonville the day before and sent texts and calls to make sure that they were able to go to the club that Queenie strong-armed and had rebuilt after she blew it up. With it in her name, her girls were able to do whatever they wanted to do and hang loose for a change.

Kalie had applied for Spring courses at FAU and was accepted. Sheena had moved in with Legend, and they were looking for a house. Finally, she had the chance to meet the hard nose of a mother-in-law that she had been waiting to meet. The only thing that offended her when meeting the woman, who was almost six-feet even, was the fact that she had to ask Legend if she was a Negro and told her son that it was his funeral if he wanted to proceed but she would support him. Unbelievably, she had been nothing short of nice to Sheena.

Mocha, on the other hand, really let loose and chugged down drinks over the fact that Calmly replaced her ring and gave her a whole room in his home where she could lounge. A private place to call her own. He even agreed to have a sit-down with his mother to discuss a custody arrangement dealing with his nephew so that Mocha could get into the swing of having a new baby. Though Samuel was special needs, Calmly had the chance to see what could soften hard Mocha. It was children. What he wanted to talk to her about all that time was letting Samuel around her so that he could get used to her. It worked, evidently. Samuel loved Mocha and would hate for Calmly, or Tio Lito as he called him, to interrupt their play time whenever Calmly's mother would bring him by.

Sitting at the bar, Kalie bobbed her head to the loud music while sipping her drink. Dressed in a short, black, leather dress, she crossed her legs and turned to the dance floor to see all of the partygoers enjoying themselves. One particular man who was making his way through the crowd caught her attention. His long, silky braids hung over both his shoulders, and as usual, he was shirtless. Knowing his pull, he was able to get into the night spot even if he was in his drawers. Legend made his way through the close people and threw Kalie a salute when he looked up and saw her. She returned a smile, pointing to where he could find Sheena dancing with some random older gentleman who appeared to be loaded. She could tell with the way his outdated dance moves weren't as smooth as everyone else's, and his face and bald head were glistening.

She then looked up at the VIP. Mocha was overlooking the crowd when Calmly's hands slipped around her tiny, bare waist, and his lips met her cheek. Although Kalie enjoyed her sisters' love in the moment, she felt sort of left out. For a while, she scanned the crowd to see where her hard-ass man was, but there was no sign of him. She finished her drink while looking for him, and still nothing. Finally, she placed her glass down on the bar and slid off her stool while holding the end of her dress down. As soon as she took a step forward, it was almost as if the crowd had parted just for her.

With his Miami Dolphins fitted cap pulled low over his eyes and his wrist held at his center, he tilted his head with a smirk across his thick lips. "Where are you goin'?" he asked her over the music. "We don't get Phara from Magical's until two."

"In the morning?" Kalie's face contorted.

Scrappy licked his lips and approached his woman, wrapping his arms around her waist when he was close enough. "I want to take you somewhere," he whispered.

"We're in the cl—"

Scrappy hushed her with a touch of his lips. Soon, he had Kalie inside of his drop-top on I-95. This was the only time he left his top up, just so that Kalie wouldn't mess up her hair. She sat in the passenger's seat with her clutch on her lap, wondering where they could be going at almost midnight. It didn't occur to her that they were coming up on Alice Wainwright Park until it was almost too late when Scrappy zoomed past the sign.

"Babe—"

Scrappy placed a single finger over his lips with his eyes still on the road. He wasn't spoiling this surprise for anything in this world. His boys were already on their way back to the house to set up for her surprise welcome home as a new woman. Even Queenie was in on his wonderful work. In the morning, Kalie would even get to meet Judeline and Xavier, Scrappy's parents. When thinking of this, a full smile spread across his face.

Soon, he parked and helped her out of the car. Hand in hand they walked the land while sharing goofy memories about their childhood until they came upon two park benches that faced what looked like a stone shipwreck in the bay. The lights from the across the body of water danced and twinkled against the rolling waves. It was so beautiful that it almost took Kalie's breath away. Scrappy caught on to Kalie hugging herself; she was slightly shivering because of the icy wind coming off the water. The gentleman he was, Scrappy took off his white and green plaid button-up and draped it over her shoulders. Then, without letting her thank him, he slipped down to one knee.

Kalie covered her mouth as tears welled in her eyes. "Scrap—"

"*Edwin*," he corrected her with a smile as he pulled a box from his back pocket.

Even though she was cold, Kalie had to fan herself. She couldn't believe that the moment was happening.

"I came to this place once when I was threatening to kill myself. But it was here that I got the call telling me that I would be a father. Tamara thought I would think she was lying, so she sent me a video of her in the examination room and zoomed in on the screen where they were giving her a sonogram. I felt like I could live again on that day. I realized that I had no choice but to keep on living for my seed. Then, there was you." Opening the box, Scrappy had to clear his throat. He had instantly become choked up when thinking of their happiness. "Kay... you and I know that I don't have it all. Somehow with you, I feel like I do. Mentally and emotionally, I am complete. My family is complete. We're even bringing a baby into this world, and I am more than happy that it's with someone who is so stable and sturdy. Someone who my daughter completely adores and loves. Someone who, not only puts my best interest at heart, but hers too. Kalie, you came into my life when everything seemed so dark and lonesome, when everything seemed like it was too hectic for me to deal with, and you rode with me. You rode hard, baby. Just like with Phara, I believe I can keep on living. But with because of you. *With* you. I just want to know, after all of that, if you would be willing to let me make you happy for the rest of our lives."

Kalie animatedly nodded as her tears flowed. "Yes, Edwin. Yes, I'll marry you."

Scrappy tenderly grabbed her left hand and slipped a white gold ring onto her finger. It was a two carat, round center, single solitaire diamond, held in place by six knife-edge prongs. It was well crafted on a fourteen karat, white gold band. He figured that since she adored the simple things, that the ring he bought over a month ago when fearing that she would leave him would do him a justice. Even though the whole wedding set cost him roughly $10,000, he was still sure that she would appreciate it.

With a gentle kiss to the back of her hand as a stray tear rolled down his cheek, he honestly felt more than alive. He could feel the rhythm of his heart.

Scrappy helped Kalie out of the car in the driveway of his home. She couldn't stop crying. Every time she looked down at her ring, she would have a random set of tears to swell and spill over. As soon as Scrappy opened the front door, the crew screamed, "Congratulations!" It scared the hell out of her.

"Where did y'all park?" she nervously laughed.

"Behind the house. Duh!" Legend was the first to wrap his arms around her for a decent hug. "Welcome, officially, to the family. Wait... You said yes, right?"

Kalie held her hand up when he pulled away to show him the ring that he knew she was getting. "Of course, I said yes!"

"Congrats, honey." Mocha kissed her sister's cheek and handed her a flute of red wine since it was the only thing that she could drink while being pregnant.

Calmly was next to peck both her cheeks and slap hands with his boy. "We know Haitians don't really have engagement parties, so this is as close as you're going to get."

"Oh, and don't worry about Phara. We're going to go and get her from Magical's."

"Are you sure?" Kalie asked skeptically. "We're going to go and get her. It's no bother."

"This bitch," she said to Calmly. "This is the shit that I'm talkin' about, baby. Both these bitches want to baby-hog and shit. We need to rent one from somewhere."

"We can't rent no baby, Mo. Bring your crazy ass on so I can get some sleep." Calmly pulled her by the hand to leave the house.

Sheena approached her sister with a grin and kissed her cheek. "I'm very happy for you, Kay. And, Scrappy, you better make my sister happy. Don't make me pop up on you."

"I won't," he chuckled.

After she and Legend closed the gate, Scrappy locked it and closed the door to secure the deadbolt. "Baby," he said as he turned. "This is just the beginning."

CHAPTER SIXTEEN

Say It One More Time

*W*hen Kalie rolled over, Phara's hair was in her face. She must've been sleepwalking or something when they retrieved her because she didn't remember seeing the little darling at all before now. She brushed Phara's long locks away from her face and gave her a kiss on the cheek that woke her. Behind her, Scrappy's spot was ice cold. He hadn't been in bed for a while. Kalie ignored it and urged Phara to follow her so that they could perform their morning routine to get themselves together.

When reaching the master bath, she saw that Scrappy had already hung a denim skirt and a white cotton shirt with a deep v-shaped neckline. Her white, low-top Chuck Taylors were sitting on the counter alongside Phara's.

With joy, she bathed the little one and had her brushing her teeth and washing her face while Kylie, herself, quickly showered. Then, she grabbed her robe and slipped it on before coming out of the shower so that she could get Phara dressed and groomed, having her to standby and teach her a few lines of Haitian-Creole while she readied herself for the day. With minimal makeup applied and her and her stepdaughter looking grand, she finally left the room to see what Mr. Broadus could've been up to. The clock on the nightstand gleamed that it was nine in the morning. She could smell his musky scent in the air when walking through the master bedroom. He was up to something indeed.

Nervously, she traveled down the hall to find a few young men leaving out of the front door.

"Thank y'all." Scrappy appeared from the other side of the wall with a stack of money in his hand. Equally he divided the bills and handed them out. "Don't forget to come back by eleven. Tell Mrs. Alexander I said thanks for the food."

"No prob, Scrappy." The tallest of the bunch dapped him up. "Don't forget to tell her what day you guys are marrying on. My mama would love to be there."

"You know I'm stickin' to tradition. I just think that the majority of the community is just happy that I'm not going to marry—"

"Shhh!" The man placed his finger at his lips. "You know that it's bad luck to bring up an ex's name."

"We're Haitian," Scrappy chuckled. "Everything we do outside of tradition is considered bad luck."

The men exchanged a handshake before they parted, leaving Scrappy to throw a salute at the other two. As he was about to close the door, the woman with his features stepped up on the porch with a smile, dressed in white to symbolize a new beginning.

Scrappy couldn't help but to expose his gold teeth and open his arms to her. He and Judeline had long buried the hatchet, and to prove so, he had invited her and Xavier to the family breakfast. When Scrappy pulled away, he leaned outside to look for his father. Not seeing him at all, he gulped and closed the door.

Judeline squealed when seeing Phara standing there in the hall. She readily assumed that she was the granddaughter that she had heard so much about. She squatted in her white skinny jeans and spread her arms for the little one. "Hey, Phara," she greeted her. "I'm Grandma Judy. I'm your papa's mom."

Phara looked back and up at Kalie, and then back at Judeline with an uneasy expression donning her cherubic face. "Bonjour, Grand-mère."

The woman clasped her hands over her mouth when hearing her granddaughter's French. She looked back at her proud son over her shoulder with tears in her eyes.

Scrappy shrugged with his teeth still exposed and the corners of his mouth raised.

Then, Judeline took her misty eyes to grinning Kalie.

"She speaks French or Creole when she's unsure of you or either when she's nervous," Kalie informed her.

"And you are the amazing Kalie Devieux I've heard so much about." Judeline's tears spilled over when she stood to hug Kalie. "I'm so grateful to be a part of this," she lightly giggled over her daughter-in-law's shoulder. She pulled away with an even wider smile, saying, "You're so beautiful!"

"Thank you, Ms. Judy."

A vicious knock came at the front door, followed by, "Hey! Y'all better open this door!"

Scrappy pulled the door open to see Queenie standing there in her blue jean capris and clinging white blouse. Her large white designer bag hung from her wrist with her free hand pressed into her hip.

"Now, I know I'm only two minutes late, but you didn't have to lock me out, Mr. Broadus," she joked. "You come over here and hug my neck, you incredible man, you!"

Happily, Scrappy leaned over to wrap his arms around Queenie's shoulders.

"Ooh, and you smell so good! What's that you got on?"

He pulled away, informing her, "Dior Sauvage."

"Ooh, Mommy likes that. *Adore the wild.* Yes! Hello!" she then spoke to Judeline. "How are you? I'm Queenie. I'm Kalie's mother. You are?"

"Judeline," she responded. "Edwin's mother."

Queenie closely eyed the woman. She just knew that she recognized her from somewhere. She just couldn't put her finger on it. "Aren't we dolled up this morning? I love that pant suit. Who's your tailor?"

"Her name is Shaniqua. She lives in Gainesville. You wouldn't know her."

Queenie tossed her head back to laugh off the shade that Judeline threw her way. "With a name like Shaniqua and with her living in Gainesville, I'm more than sure I wouldn't know her, dear. Where's the food? When will we start talking about this planning?"

"Morning!" Mocha cheered as she galloped through the front door, looking a little more than refreshed. The first person she hugged was Scrappy, then her mother, and finally picking up Phara off her feet to smother her little cheeks in kisses.

"What's up, everybody?" Calmly greeted the bunch with his white Nike golfing cap pulled low over his brow to hide the dark circles around his eyes. He hugged his kin, and then was introduced to Judeline. He could feel the tension between her and Queenie and sensed the jealousy from Judeline.

"Boy, if you don't move," Sheena threatened him when she entered. "Hey!" she screamed at Mocha. "You hand over my niece! Drop her and nobody gets hurt."

"Bullshit! I call dibs, homie!" Legend moved Sheena out of the way and snatched Phara away from Mocha.

"Babe!" she screamed. "You gonna let him do that to me? He just kidnapped the baby!"

Calmly innocently shrugged.

"You missed Uncle?" Legend sang as he bounced her on his arm. "Yea, you missed me. You don't want to be with all these ugly, mean, and nasty people."

Phara grabbed Legend's cheeks and kissed his nose with a smile.

"Oh, okay," Sheena said as she dug in her purse that was spending from her wrist. "Oh, I know what's gonna get her over here." Suddenly, Sheena pulled out a hundred-dollar bill and waved it in the air. "Now do you want Auntie Shee-Shee?"

Phara shook her head.

"Cooold blooded," Legend sang.

"Boy!" Queenie called him. "Put Princess Phara down and come hug your mother-in-law. I'm kind of jealous that everybody else done hugged me and you're all over."

Instead of putting Phara down, he kept her on his arm so that Sheena couldn't get her. He obliged Queenie anyhow, then took a step away.

"Now that Mommy's gotten all her hugs, come on so we can eat. That is unless we're waiting for someone else." She cut her eyes at Judeline, insinuating that they were all going to wait for a husband of some sort.

Scrappy clasped his hands together to break the silence in the room. "Y'all, let's go eat!"

After the last fork dropped beside the plate, the group was still laughing it up over one of Queenie's walks down memory lane. Legend had gotten out of his seat from the table that the young men had placed in the living room after storing Scrappy's other front room furniture in a shed across from his pool. Their mother, Mrs. Alexander, had catered breakfast for the crew and was working on dinner for Scrappy and Kalie. Legend took the reign of whipping up a lunch for their half day celebration. He took his time to pour up a few more mimosas and split chicken breast in half so that he could get ready to stuff them with bread crumbs and cheese.

"Oh, baby, let me help you," Queenie offered as she rose from her seat at the table. "You shouldn't have to do that alone."

"Nah, it's cool, Ma," he chuckled. "I got it in here. You relax."

"You sure? Sheena, go and help your man. Don't just sit there. He had to work yesterday."

Sheena rolled her eyes. "Mommy, trust me. Legend will mess your head up with his cooking. He got it. The kitchen is *his* domain. Hell, Calmly's kitchen too, when Mocha ain't in it."

"Damn straight!" Mocha commented. "*When* Ms. Mocha ain't in the kitchen. Legend is always showin' up to hang but end up in everybody's kitchen."

"Well, alright," Queenie softly said as she sat. "So, what about this wedding? What's the budget?"

Judeline cleared her throat. "I believe my son mentioned that it will be strictly traditional."

"Oh, and I've been looking up your traditions online, Scrappy. How are you going to do your parade to the church? Have you chosen a church?"

"Actually—"

Judeline cut off her son. "They were engaged just last night. Of course he hasn't chosen a church. He proposed *just last night*."

"I believe I was speaking to Scrappy," Queenie said with a smile.

"And I believe I was speaking to you."

"Judy, what's your issue with me?"

"My issue is that you walked off into my son's home a little too excited for my liking. Everyone was so loud and… and—"

"Country?" Mocha asked her with a cocked brow. "Well, you will have to excuse us for actually giving a damn about happiness, and for being completely overjoyed that our little sister and daughter is marrying a good man whom we all trust. Quite frankly, Judy, I don't like your attitude. You're the only one not laughing or having a good time, and your nose is stuck a little too far into the air for my liking. Lastly, instead of trying to shove something so traditional down everybody's throats, you could've asked if we knew anything about the Haitian heritage. In actuality, we do. Scrappy's been around us long enough for us to know the holidays and celebrations. He's the man of the house, and it's important in this engagement for him to take the floor, not you. Now look who's stepping outside of *tradition*."

Sheena leaned over the table to give her sister a high-five for that last remark.

"Well." Judeline stood and fetched her purse from the floor beside her chair. "Edwin, when you're done canoodling then you know where to find me."

"What?" He looked up at her with his brows together. For a split second, he allowed her to see the little boy in him that missed her; he tried to bury that deep inside. When he blinked, the child was again earthed and presented now a man. An angry one. "Why are you leaving?"

"I tried to swallow the fact that she wasn't Haitian, yet, you sit here in your own home and let these people belittle me."

"Belittle you?"

"As I've said. You know where to find me when you're done here."

Legend gently grabbed Judeline's shoulders with both hands and sat her right back down in her seat. "Listen, lady," he said firmly. "My bro done been through a lot without you, and I'll be damned if you walk out on him just to try and guilt-trip him. This here is a family. A real one. We don't walk out on each other. We handle shit like adults. Even when it hurts. Now smile, enjoy your son, and thank God that he's not marrying the bitch he had before Kalie, who is a mixed Afro-American with Cuban." With a pat to the shoulder, he returned to his kitchen duties with a smirk.

"So," Kalie spoke. "What is it that you do for a living, Mama Judy?"

She cut her eyes at Kalie before taking them to a glass that she picked up. Swirling her mimosa around, she responded, "I'm in the investment banking business, honey."

"Lies," Queenie retorted.

"Excuse me?" she scoffed.

"Girl, straight facts. I remember who you are. They used to call you Big Booty Judy. You never could keep your hoe ass at home. You got your fat ass under the right man's nose, and he got you onto money laundering. I didn't want to say nothin' at this table until you started tootin' your nose up at every-damn-thing."

"Mommy," Kalie hissed across the table.

"Shut it!" Scrappy yelled. "Obviously, this wasn't a good idea to try to get everybody under one roof to try and celebrate a little happiness. Why does it have to be dig for dig when this day isn't about either of you? Take shots at each other outside because I'm not about to hear this. Both of y'all can go. There's the front door."

Queenie rolled her eyes. "I am not leaving my son-in-law's house because his deadbeat mama decided to open her cocksuckers and speak against me."

Sheena spat out her drink.

"How dare you?" Judeline asked breathlessly. She was truly insulted. "You know nothing about me, you… you… *harlot!*"

"I'm a *retired* hoe, not a harlot. Get it straight."

"Jezebel! Mary Magdalene in the flesh!"

Mocha slammed her glass onto the table. "Uhh! Ain't nothin' wrong with hoein' as long as you gettin' your money up front and you're staying protected!"

"Well, it figures that you would teach your girls to drop to their knees for quarters!"

Queenie leaned back in her seat as she grabbed her handbag from the floor. "Oooh! She talkin' about my babies. Now I got to cut her."

As soon as Queenie stood, flipping her switchblade, Judeline jumped out of her seat and tried to move out of the way. She ended up tripping over Calmly, who was sitting right next to her, and pushed him out of the way to avoid getting sliced in the moment.

Kalie grabbed Phara when she noticed her standing in the archway of the hall and picked her up so that she wouldn't get trampled.

"Are y'all fuckin' serious?" Scrappy screamed as he banged his fists on the table.

Everyone in the living room halted.

"This is supposed to a happy moment for me and Kalie, and y'all got to lose y'all fuckin' minds!"

Judeline threw her hands up. "They're trying to kill me—"

"And you? I really wanted you to be a part of this, but you had to come here with your nose in the air. This woman, this family, has been nothing but good to me. You haven't been here in a many of moons, but you want to pass judgement? Why couldn't this be about me? Don't you think you owe me that? Just to finally be there for *me*?"

"These people are dangerous, Edwin. It's not what I want for you."

Scrappy slowly drug his hand down his face. "You really have no idea who I am, Judy. That, mother, is the saddest part of this whole ordeal. Leave."

"Edwin—"

"Go. Just get out." He plopped down in his seat with his palm resting against his forehead.

"Honey, I—"

"What part don't you understand?" he grumbled. "I still don't know you after all this time, and you still don't know me. I want to keep it that way. Now, leave. The rest of y'all, too. Me and my girls need our alone time. *Please*."

Kalie pulled Phara's head into her shoulder so that she couldn't see the pained look on her father's face. "Thank you all for coming to breakfast. Don't forget to call us when you make it home."

Mocha clicked her tongue. "Now that is a classy way to throw somebody out. Gone 'head, Baby K. C'mon, y'all. Let's get out of here. Let's leave the Broaduses to themselves."

Legend patted Scrappy's shoulder as he passed to exit the house. "Kay, take that chicken out of the oven in about thirty minutes. A second later and you'll have burned cheese."

She nodded while he walked out with the rest of the group.

"Kay, I'm so sorry," Queenie apologized. "It wasn't my intention to ruin things, but she had it coming."

"Mommy, sometimes, you should let me handle things, alright? I heard the shade, I got stung with venom, and I saw her reactions just like you did. Scrappy and I could've handled it."

"Speaking of which, tell your man I'm truly sorry. I know he wants to blow up right now."

"Knowing him, he just might."

Queenie kissed hers and Phara's cheek before leaving.

When everyone was cleared out, she noticed that Scrappy was no longer seated at the table. That quickly, he had gone out of the back door and around to the garage. Kalie held herself together by locking up the house and having Phara to help her load the dishes. She and Scrappy would have to have a heart to heart when he returned.

CHAPTER SEVENTEEN

Out With The Old, In With The New

*I*t was almost eight at night by the time Scrappy had come in. Phara had already eaten, bathed, and had tired herself out. Kalie put her in her pajamas and brushed her long locks before putting her in bed. Then, she went into the kitchen to grab herself a glass of red wine so that she could finally relax. She could understand that Scrappy was all too upset to stay, but the least he could've done was call.

Kalie's phone lit up on the coffee table. She saw it when she rounded the couch to take a seat, so she grabbed it up and answered for Ms. Jackson with a smile. "Hello, Ms. Jackson," she greeted her. "What has you calling so late?"

"Hey, honey. I was wondering if you needed any help with the wedding plans. It's all a buzz in Little Haiti that our dear prince is getting married. Are you happy?"

"Very much so," Kalie gushed. "I have a beautiful daughter, an incredible man, and add a solitaire diamond on that and you've got the most happy woman alive over here."

"I bet," Ms. Jackson laughed. "I heard that you met Judy today."

Kalie took a deep breath. Just hearing about the visit left a sour taste in her mouth.

"I want to apologize for her. That woman ain't right in the head. I also heard that the only reason she came back in the first place was to try and get some money out of our Scrappy. Let that witch burn and keep her away from him, you hear me? I don't buy her bleeding heart story at all about how she so-called found him on Instagram. She was a damn good con woman. As a matter of fact, she conned Xavier out of his inheritance right after she married him. The only stipulation was that she had to be married for five years, and so—"

"She got the money and hauled ass when Scrappy was four," Kalie said with eyes as wide as saucers. "She only had him to try and prove that she was all in for the marriage."

"No, no, honey. This is why you need to let me tutor you about our culture before you get married into it. You see, after you marry, you have to be fruitful. You can stop having kids after you get your first born son. That's what she did. She left him and Xavier behind after she wiped his bank account clean."

Hearing the front gate open, Kalie jumped off the couch, saying, "Ms. Jackson… I'm going to call you back." After that, she hung up with her heart beating a million miles per minute.

Through the door came her man, as sober as he was ever going to be, without a wrinkle in his clothes. The pair locked eyes for what felt like forever until Scrappy looked to the floor as he closed the front door behind him.

"Baby, I'm sorry about today," Kalie offered. "I knew I should've counseled with you guys to make sure that everything was going to fall into place. I'm never going to make that mistake again. I knew I should've—"

"It wasn't you," he mumbled. Slowly, he inched into the living room where the Alexander boys had already returned and took the table away, placing his furniture back where it belonged. Scrappy took a seat on the couch with Kalie, lying his head in her lap. "I met up with her a few hours ago, and she asked me for ten grand."

"Baby, that's because—"

"That's what she does," he quietly admitted. "I signed my dad out today, had a talk with him, and took him to the flat where my mama's staying. Their words for each other weren't quite as beautiful as ours are to each other, but she confessed to what she did. She didn't really love him. She just wanted his money. In turn, she didn't love me either." Scrappy choked up at the end of his sentence. He folded his arms over his chest as he let those words burn a hole in his heart. "But it's okay," he continued with a sniffle. "I know where the root of my confusion comes from, and nothing is more clear to me than the fact that I'm ten times better than any one of them will ever be. That includes me being a damn good parent."

Kalie giggled then.

"What's funny?" He looked up at her with serious eyes.

"Your baritone makes the baby move," she explained. "It's this weird flutter in my stomach; like it knows who you are."

"It should." Scrappy rolled over to kiss her belly through her long t-shirt. "It will always know that daddy is right here, loves them, and isn't going anywhere for any amount of money in this world."

"Babe, don't do that," she laughed. "It tickles when the baby moves."

Scrappy kissed her small pudge again and rested his head over her legs. "I'm sorry about walking out on you, Kay. I was just so angry—"

"I know. And besides… I'm just happy your mama left. She was about to get sliced up and two pieced around this place. But I'm glad that you tried, Edwin. That's what real men do. I'd rather take that than you flipping over the dinner table." Lovingly, she kissed his cheek as she stroked his long sideburns. "Oh, Mrs. Alexander sent out dinner. It's all stacked up in the oven."

"Phara eat?"

"I'm her mother, Scrappy. Of course, I fed her."

"Well then…" He rolled off the couch and pulled his woman up by her hand. "Let's go feed our other baby. These hunger pains ain't no joke. I don't miss these motherfuckers at all."

Kalie kissed him softly on the lips. To her, they were in a much better place, and nothing and no one had the power to change that.

One month later and Mocha stirred on top of the cold sheets of her and Calmly's brand new king-sized bed. Having him working harder than ever when getting the new strip club was not at all an enjoyable experience for her. He never wanted her to work; he'd rather for her to lounge or enjoy her time. Mocha was used to grinding. Being a housewife was exciting at first, but she needed a thrill.

She groomed herself and had done her makeup to perfection before styling her expensive lace front wig. She loved how the edges were solid black and flared into platinum blond at the tips. She knew that Calmly loved it, too. With it nearing Christmas, Mocha had shopping to do and a wedding to plan. Not just for Kalie but for her own.

After pulling on a clinging, black, long sleeved shirt, skinny jeans, black, leather, thigh-high boots, and a black, leather jacket, she was off to the mall where she would eventually sucker Dolla into meeting her there. Unfortunately for her, when she called him, the voice she heard on the other end was not that of the man she was expecting to hear from.

Mocha swallowed and backed away from the door with her eyes narrowed. "How the fuck are you still alive?" she asked Bandz.

"Well," he chuckled, "you were sloppy. How else would I still be alive, Mocha Latte?"

"Where the fuck is Dolla?"

"He should be turning around very shortly. He should've figured out by now that he's left his phone at the house. What are you wearing?"

"Don't fuck with me, *rapist*."

"You shouldn't fuck with yourself, *murderer*. Or... shall I call you an *attempted* murderer?"

"Sonofabitch, if I ever catch you in public—"

"You never will. And you might want to lay low because it's around the time for you to cough up my nephew. Or is it *my* son? Whichever one, my brother's coming for the kid. You really fucked up when you tried to kill me. You know he's going to put a bullet in your head after you spit that baby out, right? Well… he might get to that nigga, Calm, first. I heard y'all are all booed up now. Even my baby, Kalie. Don't you worry about Scrappy. I'll take care of him myself."

"Bandz, you pathetic motherfucker… you forgot that a bitch like me doesn't live in fuckin' fear."

As if what she had said was comical, Bandz burst into laughter and hung up on the woman.

Mocha squeezed her phone in her hand. She didn't like for someone to have a one up on her, so she did the only thing she could. She called her brother-in-law, Scrappy. She remembered Kalie, in the middle of a random rant not too long ago, mention how she had to spare Tamara's life because she threw out the fact that Phara was Bandz's biological daughter. If anybody, other than her, wanted to get rid of Bandz, then it was him.

"Hello?" he answered in a raspy voice.

"Hey, little brother," she greeted him with a smile as though he could see her. "Were you still asleep?"

"The streets don't feed themselves at night. Of course, I was still asleep. What's good?"

"Tamara. I need you to get some information out of her. And when you do, I need you to find Bandz. It's lights out for him. You leave Dolla to me. He's nothing but my mother's pet and a gas money provider. Make sure you take the rest of the Flockas with you. I want to make sure he's dead and gone this time."

"What you mean, this time?"

"I mean that..." Mocha wasn't about to incriminate herself by fessing up to trying to kill the poor boy. "Well... Kalie told me that you set fire to the mansion. So... yeah. One would assume you were trying to kill them both."

"Consider it done." Scrappy hung up, leaving Mocha to smile inside.

Then, she called her mother. She needed tabs on her bitch so that she could go ahead and finish him off. "Mommy?" she said after Queenie answered. "Are you meeting with your boy today?... Good. Don't tell him that I'm coming to make my final visit."

CHAPTER EIGHTEEN

Ain't Over Until It's Over

With it being payday, Dolla retrieved his phone from his home and strutted into the foyer of Queenie's. Wearing black gloves, a pair of slacks, and a white dress shirt, he pleasantly closed the office doors to have a private word with the woman.

Queenie was wrapping up a phone call when he entered, holding her pointer finger in the air for him to hold on. Impatient, Dolla pulled his pistol from the front of his trousers. Queenie continued her conversation with her eyes on the silencer screwed onto the nozzle of the gun. He didn't scare her any, though she knew that he meant business.

"Alright, love. I'll write that down. Talk to you later." Still dressed in her workout attire, she hung up her phone and grabbed her pen to jot down her notes inside her composition notebook. "I see you came strapped today," she mentioned to Dolla. "Any particular reason why that is?"

"Where's my kid, Queenie?" he asked her. "You didn't have a lavish baby shower, a welcome home party, and your kids damn sure ain't been back over here since the dinner. Tell me what the fuck is up with my baby, man."

She dropped her pen and leaned back in her chair that resembled a throne. Her eyes were soft as she crossed her legs to stare at him, showing him that she was completely unbothered. "My kids aren't your concern, William. Your money should be. Although, I do know that you've been making money off the club on Collins, and since they've closed down, you've been pretty much starving and waiting for my scraps. Sad to say that my son-in-law, Calmly, owns that place now, and he'll be opening it up pretty soon. Did you honestly think that the Queen didn't know about your extra sideline gigs? Did you honestly think that I wouldn't be waiting on this day that you would slither into some part of my home and try to kill me?"

Dolla opened his mouth to say something, yet all he could do was yelp like an injured dog after feeling a sharp pain on the back of his head. He fell to the floor, dropping his gun. For a second, his senses were knocked unconscious. Through blurred vision, a pointed toe of a boot kicked his gun out of reach and a set of stiletto nails dug into his jaws to turn his face toward a beautiful, yet angry, woman.

"I've been waiting, Dolla," Mocha told him with a smile. "For seven long years, I've been waiting for the day that you would have to crawl to me. But I will make an exception, this time since you're lying there like the limp dick that you are."

Without another word, Mocha used the bottom of the lamp that she had already used to whack her ex with and disfigured his face while opening a hole in his cranium. With how quickly she bashed his skull in, he didn't have time to react or scream. Had she not practiced fucking him up on her old Mercedes, he could've actually had a chance at fighting back.

When she was done, Mocha threw the lamp across the room with her chest heaving. "You don't tell my man about this," she said to her mother out of breath. "I will come and sleep in your bed before I have to hear about all that other bullshit."

"I'm not saying a damn thing because the only motherfucker sleeping between my sheets is me. Let me get somebody in here to clean this shit up."

"Thanks, Ma. I have to call my sisters so we can go shopping. No one is to know that I was here. The last thing I want is to argue with Calmly about how I was so called stressing when I wasn't."

"About that—"

Queenie was cut off by the ringing of Mocha's phone inside her front pocket. It was Calmly's ringtone.

Mocha looked over at her mother with a tilted head. But there was no way that Queenie could've called her son-in-law. She pulled her phone out and answered. "Hey, babe."

"Where you at?" he asked her.

His roughness made her inner thighs tingle. "I'm out. Was thinking of going shopping in a little bit."

"You pretty little liar. Get your ass to this house. Scrappy called me about us needing to go see Bandz. He say you gave him the permission. I want you and the girls in the house until we finish up tying these loose ends."

"Okay, baby," she said with a pout.

"What did you do?"

"What?" she asked with a shocked tone.

"You're pouting and shit. Mo, what the fuck have you done?"

"Babe, I—"

"Didn't I tell you I was gonna see about that nigga, Dolla, myself?"

"I didn't—"

"I'm lookin' at your GPS on Maps, Mo! You ain't got no reason to be at your mama's house when he's there! Today is payday, and everybody know that shit. Get your motherfuckin' ass to this house with your hardheaded ass! I swear to God, if you done fucked up a chance at us having another baby, girl—"

"Okay, Calmly, damn! I'm comin'!"

"With yo' crazy ass! You gon' make me fuck around and choke the shit out of you! And not in the way you like it either. Get the fuck to the house! We gotta go and pick up the keys to the new house and your ass is out here doin' shit that you ain't got no business doin'! Swear fo' God if we go Monday morning to get you a pregnancy test and you ain't pregnant—"

"What that got to do with anything?"

"We've been trying to have a baby, but your ass wanna stress about everything under the motherfuckin' sun! And what about you going to see Baby K about grieving and shit? That means all her hard work goes to waste, too, 'cause you here goin' to see about niggas!"

"No, it doesn't."

"It *does*. Get yo' ass in the house, girl!"

Mocha rolled her eyes and stomped her foot at the sound of him hanging up on her. She couldn't believe that somebody was able to tie a leash around her neck finally.

Queenie laughed as she finally stood from behind her desk.

"And what the fuck is so funny?" She whirled her head around to her mother as she combed her long, virgin hair to the back with her fingertips.

"Somebody finally marryin' my crazy ass Mocha. That's what's so funny. Now do what your man said before you end up in trouble."

"That ain't funny," she whined. "Let me get out of here. Don't forget that we're linking up tomorrow night with Kay about the last-minute plans and to help her pack the rest of their things."

"I know, I know." Queenie sat back down while watching her daughter storm out of her office.

A smile spread across her face when she thought of how Mocha was happy, and how Kalie was having a baby and was getting married on top of moving to Boca Raton. Sheena and her mother-in-law seemed to be getting better acquainted, and Queenie hoped that Legend would pop the question soon. The dead motherfucker on her office floor was a reminder of how far they all had come since Kalie's return. For her baby girl to marry a man that her mother completely trusted set Queenie at ease. She could freely breathe, knowing that her daughters were properly taken care of.

———————

"Thanks, Tamara," Scrappy said as he ended the call. He pulled from his Newport just before Legend dipped inside his car.

"What she say?" Legend asked his boy.

"1901 Southwest 5th Avenue." Scrappy cranked up his car just as Calmly snapped the top of his gun in the backseat.

They were all done playing around with Bandz. All of them were in no mood to toy with him on this day. With Scrappy and Kalie's wedding right around the corner before their move, they needed to drop dead weight before they continued with their lives.

Scrappy had to blink twice when seeing the ugly house that it only took him five minutes to pull around to. His GPS had to be playing tricks on him. Bandz and Dolla would never purchase a home that didn't look sophisticated. This abode looked too normal for either of them to step foot in, yet he chucked it up to them possibly wanting to be incognito. Still, he drove through the alleyway and stopped right behind the house. The men got out and took their regular formations, only Scrappy and Calmly switched positions. Calmly would go in first.

When Calmly approached the back door, something was off to him. He tilted his head as he stared at the doorknob and pulled his cell phone from his pocket. He called his boys on a conference call so that they wouldn't be too loud when speaking.

"What's up?" Legend asked him.

"This was a little too fuckin' easy, and it's a little too goddamn quiet," he said honestly. His gut was turning flips.

Scrappy eyed the side door as he peeked in through the small window there. He didn't see any movement or anything indicating that anyone was inside. "I'm with you on that one, Calm. We should just come back. Something don't feel right about this shit. A slimy motherfucker like Bandz wouldn't just sit and wait for his death. When y'all went to see this nigga, y'all had to drag him out of bed. When I went to see him, I had to wake him up. I think this fool is up to something. Got to be."

"Besides, it's too light out," Calmly told them as he backed away from the door.

Legend stepped away from the oddly placed doormat when he heard a click. It was so loud that the other two heard it over and outside of their call.

"The fuck was that?"

"Nigga, run!" Scrappy alerted him.

All three retreated to the car with their thoughts racing a million miles per second. Scrappy knew what that sound was. Most members of the Haitian Mafia used devices as such; just to quickly get rid of a nemesis without a trace. It was a trigger that Legend stepped on to detonate a bomb. What Bandz thought was going to happen was that someone, even his brother, Mocha, or Tamara, would stand there long enough to figure out what they had stepped on, and by the time they figured it out, everything would explode.

Legend hopped a fence on the side of the house and ran across the street until he could hear the screech of Scrappy's tires. Just before he could hop into the car, everyone on the block could hear a loud boom, followed by the feeling of the ground shaking.

Thick clouds of black smoke surrounded the city block. They were so thick that they didn't let up until sirens were soaring through the air. Nosy neighbors had come out of their damaged homes to see what could've happened in that instant, only finding a classic car turned over onto its side, wrapped around a street pole, and three disfigured bodies sprawled out onto the street.

CHAPTER NINETEEN

Almost A Little Too Late

Sheena laughed after Kalie had basically punked the hell out of Mocha into giving her a popsicle when she knew that Scrappy would have a fit over her sugar intake for the baby.

"I don't care," Mocha angrily said as she combed Kalie's locks up into a ponytail in the dining room. "Those are Carlito's. He'll have somebody else to be mad at other than me. Fuck him. He's always tryin' to dig in my ass over small shit."

Sheena bent over the table to stick her butt out in her skintight jeans. "You know you like it," she laughed as she twerked.

"I do like that shit, though." Mocha stuck out her tongue.

"Wait a minute." Kalie caught a piece of flavored ice that she only thought was running down her chin, and then looked up at her oldest sister. "You do anal?"

"Hell, yea! You should too if you know what's good for you."

"But... what if something comes out?"

"It won't if you take care of yourself. See, this is why I should've been more active in your life. Proven fact. There's a nerve inside your ass that gives you an orgasm automatically. Girl, you better toot that thing up and let Scrappy have a go. Shit, with that raggedy bitch he was with, I'm pretty sure she done had it in all positions and in every single way."

"Don't be boring, Kay," Sheena laughed. "You'll be surprised during your first time. You'll bust quick as hell and have to stop for Gatorade."

"Hello!" Mocha dropped her comb and high-fived Sheena.

Kalie's cell phone rang on the table next to Sheena's elbow. She looked down at the screen, noticing that it was her mother's lawyer's number. Her brows squeezed. "What the hell is the Jew calling for?"

"I'm pretty sure he's not Hebrew," Kalie commented. "And Sheena that makes you racist."

Sheena rolled her eyes and answered her sister's phone. "What?"

"Who am I speaking with?"

"Cohen, this is Sheena. What do you want? We're having a little girl's time."

"Close out that girl's time and get down to Mercy. Edwin is awake and they're questioning him about an explosion."

"Awake?" she shrieked. "Explosion? What the fuck—"

"Listen, he lawyered up, so I'm on my way. Whatever it was had to be life threatening. Let's all be lucky that he didn't want to mumble a coerced confession of some kind. I'm on my way out there." Charles Cohen hung up to call Queenie next.

Sheena dropped Kalie's phone and grabbed her sister up out of the chair.

"What happened?" Kalie panicked.

"We got to get to Mercy. Something happened with the guys. An explosion or some shit. I'm guessing Scrappy was unconscious so that means that our men must be hurt, too. Put your damn shoes on and let's go!"

Mocha grabbed her purse out of the chair that was next to the one Kalie was snatched out of, and then she scurried into the living room to find a random pair of heels that she had taken off days prior. She wasn't in the mood to wrestle with the boots that she had just taken off.

Sheena cracked on the inside, hoping that her love wasn't gravely injured. She had something to tell him. Something more than important.

Sheena separated from her sisters and others who were gathered around when the nurses at the station were able to tell her which curtain Legend was behind. The ER was in pure mayhem with as many of the neighbors that had to go to Mercy Hospital just to get checked out. With the straps of her hand bag being clutched tight inside her fist, she had never walked so fast in her life to get to curtain number twelve. She twisted and turned in the middle aisle to see where the numbers somehow seemed to get off track.

"No! No more fucking needles!"

Sheena whirled around and quickly stomped in her heels to get to her man screaming at someone. Low and behold, she found curtain number twelve at the far end of the aisle; only, there was no card outside of the curtain. She pulled it back to find Legend in his black briefs, leaning away from a nurse. His left leg was in a splint, and they had already bandaged up the right side of his face.

"Hey!" Sheena angrily called out to the nurse. "What are you giving him?"

"It's just morphine, ma'am," the young woman responded. "He was complaining of pain after his knee was popped back into place."

"Either put it in his IV or bring him morphine pills. Can't you see that he doesn't like needles?"

"I can see that. But he also doesn't want to keep wearing his oxygen mask. He must keep it on until his lungs are clear."

"Judging by how loud he was, I'd say that you've scared the hell out of him with that big ass needle. His lungs sounded pretty clear from there. Just leave and get him pills."

"Oh my God, baby," Legend almost cried. He reached for her to come closer so that he wouldn't feel alone anymore. "She was about to stick me again. I came to when they were drawing blood. Baby, they put a needle in me."

Sheena slapped Legend's cheek and pulled his oxygen mask from the top of his head to fit it on, over his nose and mouth.

"What was that for?" His voice was muffled, but his eyes were wide and hurt.

"You don't ever scare me like that again, Legend!" she reprimanded him. "I thought that I was going to have to raise this damn baby by myself and end up planning your fucking funeral all in one!"

"Wait a minute." He lifted his mask, only for Sheena to pop his hand and readjust it. "Baby, did you say that you were raising a baby?"

"That's exactly what the hell I said, and if you would've died on me, I would've fuckin' killed you."

"But... I would already be dead, if—"

"I didn't ask you all that!"

"I'm sorry." He pulled the belt loop of her jeans to make her sit on the side of his bed, wrapping his arms around her waist. "Baby, when did you find out? Why didn't you tell me?"

"I'm late, Legend. I was supposed to get my period three weeks ago. It's not from stress, so the only thing that I could think of was that you tried to trap me into marrying you."

"Well, we've been together for a hot little minute. So, what's up?"

"Are you proposing to me?"

"I'm saying... what's up? Would you?"

"Legend—"

"Sheena, will you marry me, with your mean ass? A motherfucker almost died today, and you want to deny me basically what I'm owed?"

"Basic? Owe you? Shut the fuck up and hug me since you can't kiss me."

Legend obliged. What he didn't see was that the nurse had returned and couldn't find any morphine pills. She presented the needle to Sheena, who gave her a nod when Legend's back was to the young woman. The nurse pushed the needle inside of Legend's IV cord and was done and out of the small area before he could release his love.

"What smells like metal?" he asked Sheena before he had gone cross-eyed. Legend laid back on the bed with his mouth wide open as he rode the wave of sweet release.

She rolled her eyes and shook her head at the fact that he was not only a lightweight with medication, but he was seriously afraid of needles.

———————————

Mocha pulled back the curtains where she expected Calmly to be. There he was, in nothing but his plaid grey and red briefs on top of the sheets with an oxygen mask over his mouth and nose, his right arm in a cast and sling, and a large bandage over his right peck. She gulped as she closed the curtain behind her. He didn't move. The heart monitor that he was attached to by stickers on his chest displayed single lines scrolling across the screen. She lost her breath and her footing. She ended up kneeling beside his bed with tears pouring out of her eyes.

"Carlito," she whimpered. "What happened? What happened to you? You can't go and be with our son. I need you here, babe. I need you *here*. You got to come back to me. What about your nephew? Baby, he needs you too. God! Please. I—"

Rough coughing scared the daylights out of Mocha. She stood and jumped back from the bed as if God himself had reached down and touched her love's heart to wake him. Calmly tried to roll over but the IV and blood pressure cuff wouldn't allow him to do that. Neither did the anesthetics that were in his system. To make sure that she wasn't losing her mind indefinitely, she took her eyes to the monitor beside the bed. Still, there were single lines scrolling across the screen. That's when she noticed the setting at the bottom of the screen in bold neon orange letters telling her that the machine was placed on an idle setting.

"The fuck?" he said with a low and raspy voice, trying to lazily take off his mask.

Mocha placed her hand over her mouth and rushed back to the bed to help remove his hand from his mask. "You can't take that off," she sniffled.

"Mo, where the fuck…?"

"You're at the hospital, baby. There was something about an explosion and you guys were severely hurt."

"Explosion?"

"*Where are my babies?*" Mocha heard Queenie yell. "*Woman, if you don't get the fuck out of my face! I don't need no goddamn name tag! My babies are back here somewhere! That's clearance e-goddamn-nough!*"

She rolled her eyes and took a deep breath. "Mommy! Me and Calmly are in bed seven!"

"*Get your bony ass out of my way!*" Shortly after yelling at a nurse, she pulled the curtains apart with a look of terror on her face. "Calmly," she breathlessly called him. "Honey, are you alright?"

"I think so," he grumbled, scratching at his scalp beneath his thick, short curls. With his fingertips, he found a small line of stiches.

He was lucky to have his brain after the way he was thrown out of the car and hit his head on concrete.

"Michelle, where are the others?"

"Over here, Mommy!" Sheena shouted.

"You two hang tight. I'll be right back."

Mocha waited until Queenie whipped back the curtain to leave before she broke down again. With her fingers clasped at her forehead, she leaned over and let go of silent tears.

"Mo, come on," Calmly tried. He weakly reached for her.

"No," she whined, looking up at him. "Carlito, I thought you were gone. Do you know how it feels to fall so hard and so deep in love with someone, and then realize that you haven't expressed it how you should? Do you? Because I don't think you do! I was never worried about Dolla, and I put on a strong front like I didn't give a fuck just to avoid loving his stupid ass, but I almost puked, cried, and got a speeding ticket today. I love you so fuckin' much that I don't even know what I would do without you."

"Mo, it wasn't my fault, baby. We went over there to handle business, and shit just went wrong."

"I don't care!" she cried. "I was scared. I've never been afraid of a damn thing. Then, to know that I sent y'all to him in the first place? I took blame for losing our son, and if you would've died, that would've been on my head too. Carlito, I wouldn't have been able to live had that happened."

"Baby, I'm sorry. I didn't mean to scare you. It wasn't your fault.

It's just the code that we live by. He had it comin' so we had to do what we had to do. With how we work, there are no guarantees of any of us making it back home to begin with. Maybe you forgot that, which is why you're blaming yourself, but it ain't your fault. We're fuckin' savages, Michelle. We live this life and we die by it if we don't get out in time. That's just the way it is, baby."

"Listen, I don't want to hear about Bandz, alright? Dolla's been taken care of and you know that. Bandz will get his. Carlito, I need you. I've never said that to anybody. Baby... I... I *need* you." The end of her sentence was inaudible, but he got the message.

With his free hand, he grabbed hers and kissed it. "You'll always have me, Mo. Now straighten your face. We got us."

CHAPTER TWENTY

Hell Hath No Fury

With the Flockas being in the hospital for a few days for observation, Kalie didn't want to go home. She had to since Scrappy urged her to leave. When walking through the front door of her packed home, she stared at the Christmas tree, that Phara helped her to decorate in the corner, with tears in her eyes. She could see Scrappy before her as though he was really there with the side of his chocolate face a shade of light pink from it being burned, the gash on the side of his forehead and chin, his broken forearm in a cast, and the stitches on his thigh from where his thigh bone had snapped and the surgeons had to put it back in place. He wouldn't be getting out of the hospital for a while because he would need therapy. When the car flipped, unlike Calmly, he wasn't fortunate enough to fall directly out like Calmly did. Because of the steering wheel column, his pelvis bone fractured, and he twisted his spine which only pinched a few nerves in his back. However, when the car landed, he was blessed enough to be thrown out due to the impact of the car wrapping around the pole after the column snapped his femur. Even more so blessed, he had his life.

Kalie swallowed her tears and sat in the middle of the living room floor Indian style. With her phone in her hand and with so much rage flowing through her veins, she phoned a number that she hoped worked. She then pressed it against her ear as a single tear fell down her cheek.

"Baby, I never thought that you would call. I've missed you so much, but Scrappy tried to kill me. I told you about that. Every-fucking-day I thought about you and my baby. Please tell me that you're coming home. I want to see you and the baby. I'm tired of all of this bullshit. Come home to me, Baby K."

She could've lost the father of her unborn. She could've lost the happy husband that she so lucidly dreamed of. Instead of Scrappy walking through door and picking up Phara to swing her around, Phara would only have to sit there and constantly ask Kalie when her daddy would come back home from heaven. It enraged her. Irful, Kalie slightly shivered as she readied her words for Bandz. There was a darkness in her eyes that no one had ever seen the likes of. Darkness that Scrappy could tell her was dangerous to have.

"What's the address?" Her voice quivered as another tear fell. She didn't want to put up with him any more than anyone else did. Baby K was a baby no more.

Before Kalie left the house, she called Magical and told Phara that she loved her so much. Then, she went into her bedroom and felt around the top shelf of her closet for the pistol that she knew Scrappy concealed there. It was no secret that the maniac hid guns all over.

Afterward, she pulled on Scrappy's favorite black hoodie. Because of Bandz and what he had done, their lives would be on hold for a while. Six months, to be exact. That way, Scrappy could complete his therapy, along with pain management, and Kalie could help take care of him until he healed. She wouldn't be able to start classes until the Fall and marry around that time as well. The only plus was that Phara would be starting elementary school in a whole new area in a whole new year.

Though she was used to trying to look at the bright side of things, she couldn't. The darkness in Kalie's eyes was one that Scrappy's rage couldn't match. She slid into the black Crown Victoria and backed out of the garage with one simple mission on her mind. It was to put a stop to the last of the drama.

By the time she reached the address, she had made up in her mind that there would be no talking, there would be no pretending or faking, and she prayed to God that He would forgive her for what she was about to do.

She knocked on the door of the apartment number that he gave her, waited until he was able to see through the peephole to see who she was, and then flipped her hood up.

Bandz smirked and leaned against the pane of the door that had peeling paint on it. "Did you bring somebody with you?" he asked her in a soothing baritone.

"No," she answered lowly.

"Baby—"

He was interrupted holding up her gun with a steady wrist, and by Kalie pulling the trigger. She didn't stop unloading the clip until he was finished. She even had to step into the shabby apartment just to finish off the last round in the chamber. Standing over him to see the blood spilling out of his mouth and his hands locked in position with his wrists bent, she knew for a fact that he was gone. The very last bullet went into his skull. When she heard the subtle clicks of her pistol, indicating that there were no more bullets left, she held her breath and scurried out of the apartment, hopped inside the Ford, and drove off as though she hadn't done a thing. To her, if she sped, someone would notice her and call the police. She was thankful that the car was black on black, and that Scrappy's license plate wasn't on it.

It took her ten minutes to pull over and heave, realizing what she had done. Kalie had a complete mental breakdown when she collected the thought of taking a whole life because of drama. She gripped the steering wheel in her hand with the other hand over her belly. Kalie wailed when silently begging God to forgive her and show her mercy. She couldn't understand how the men did it because she just knew that what she had done would haunt her forever. Then there was the thought of keeping her family safe, which would somehow justify her actions as being correct.

Her cell phone rang in her back pocket, scaring the wits out of her. In a panic, she reached in and retrieved it when realizing that it was her mother's ringtone.

"Hello?" she answered, trying to use a strong voice.

"Kalie Devieux! Come and get your man!" Queenie shouted. "He doesn't want to sleep without you, but wasn't he the one to tell you to leave?"

"When did you get there?" she sniffled.

"Just a few minutes ago to check on my sons since they sent y'all home. Are you crying?"

"I'll be on my way in a sec, okay?"

Kalie didn't allow her mother to ask questions. She hung up and dropped the car off at her home, inside the garage, and then pulled off Scrappy's hoodie. She found a bandana to wrap around the gun and shoved it inside her handbag. She didn't know if she would've been able to hold up, but she knew that she would have to in order to avoid questions.

About thirty minutes after hanging up, Kalie turned the corner into Scrappy's room. As soon as she saw him again, the tears came on their own. She closed the door behind her with her foot and inched closer to his bed.

Queenie stood with a lazy hand at her chest. Chocolate, who was sitting on the other side of Scrappy's bed, took notice of the guilty look written across her face. Even she didn't expect to take time off from her restaurant to walk right into disaster.

"Baby," Scrappy lowly called her. Though he was full of morphine, he fought through it to make sure that she was okay.

She shivered as she gripped the strap of her bag.

"Baby, what's wrong? You were only angry when you left. What happened?"

Kalie pursed her lips and took tiny baby steps to her love. When she was close enough, she couldn't conceal the pain on her face. She reached into her bag and handed Scrappy the only evidence of a soon to be open murder case.

With his skinned fingers of his free hand, he grabbed it and stared at it. For a moment, thanks to his meds, he stared at the bandana, and then realized what had happened. Slowly, he took his one good eye to Queenie since his right eye temporarily had no vision.

Queenie took her cue. She walked over and grabbed the gun out of Scrappy's hand, passing it over to Chocolate. "You take that to my house and bury it underneath the roses next to the pool. Don't speak to nobody and don't tell them what you're doing. They're all supposed to be out working anyway."

Chocolate didn't utter a word. She grabbed it and shoved it into her purse on the floor beside the chair she had gotten out of, and then scurried out of the room.

Queenie grabbed her daughter's shoulders and squeezed her. "Don't speak another word of this to anybody, understand? You were protecting your family. Dry your face, Kalie."

Still shivering, she pulled away from Queenie and sat on the side of Scrappy's bed with her head hang.

"I'm going to give you two some alone time." Queenie grabbed her purse and left the room while holding her breath. She didn't think that her precious baby girl had it in her to do something so vicious.

In pain and high on medication, Scrappy wrapped his arm around his woman's waist as he leisurely rested his chin on her shoulder. He then kissed her neck. "Everything will be alright, baby," he whispered. "You're loyal, you were fed up, and you were defending your family's honor. If not, who knows what else could've happened to us all. If you didn't get him, me and the other two would have. He was already on borrowed time."

"I'm sorry," she sobbed.

"Don't be." His grip tightened, hoping that she would be okay and trusted him more than she ever had at this point. Even he was still in shock that his sweet Kalie would've been able to pull off letting a single round out of the barrel of a gun. "It only gets better from here, Kay. You hear me? Nothing but better."

CHAPTER TWENTY-ONE

Beautiful Beginnings

Six months later…

*L*egend knocked on the hotel suite door, ready to get everything over and done with. He swiped his hand over the beard he had grown, and then smoothed his short cut, curly afro with his faded sides. One last time he knocked, hoping that Scrappy would come and answer on his own.

"Psst!" Calmly leaned out of the door of his suite with Ray Bans donning his eyes.

Legend turned to him with a smirk. "That Vodka got the best of you last night?"

Calmly scratched his short curls as he closed the door behind him, and then leaned against the pane of it. "Man, we ain't ever doin' that shit again. I just brushed my teeth and had to pull my damn head out of the toilet again. Them Fireballs ain't no joke, cuddy."

Legend pointed his thumb at the door at his side. "Where the fuck is ya' boy? He ain't called to tell you that he would need help this morning?"

Calmly shook his head, having an unsettling feeling to rise within him. It could've been just another round of vomit that was threatening to spill over.

Just as Legend raised his knuckles to the door, it came open. He immediately stepped forward in case his old friend needed some assistance, yet Scrappy needed the total opposite. With his cane helping to support his weight, he took two steps outside of the door, fully dressed in his all-white tuxedo, minus the jacket. He closed the door with his last hand and adjusted the straps of his backpack on his shoulders.

He smiled at Legend, asking, "We ready to get me over that last hump?"

"Hell yeah," he laughed. "You good to walk that parade? You gon' need that cane?"

Scrappy picked it up by the neck, holding it in his hand as he smiled at it. For the last four months, he had been completely dependent upon it since being off his crutches. He wasn't going back to his wheelchair; that's just not where he was going to end up. He knew so. As the savage he was, he worked his ass off by working out before and after physical therapy and used his support to lean on his cane so that he wouldn't have to ever consider being lazy or permanently injured.

There was a twinge of pain his thigh, yet he paid no mind to it as he handed Legend the long, black stick that Queenie gifted to him for his birthday. It was a shiny, black metal with a golden crown on the top of it with his initials between several jewels that lined the headpiece.

"I won't need this today," he said pridefully. "I'm taking that four-block walk like a man. We done came too far for me to be holding on to something that I don't really need."

Legend only smirked. He looked back at Calmly and head-gestured for him to come on. Calmly grabbed his backpack and left with his boys. For him and Mocha, conceiving wasn't so easy as he thought it would be, but they were willing to take as many hormones as they needed to in order to get the kid they both wanted. Their own wedding was scheduled four months from then and both of them were happy. Among that was the permanent living situation of his nephew Samuel. Instead of split custody, he and Mocha pushed for the whole nine. That too wasn't easy since Calmly's sister was missing in action. They would either need her consent or wait six more months until the courts declared her and Calmly's mother legally inapt.

Sheena, being the hardnose she was, declared that she would get married a year after Legend had given her a ring. Finding something so perfect for her was difficult, which is what took him all of four months to find the right ring. It turned out that she wasn't pregnant after all, but they were still hopeful. Sheena figured that it was a blessing because it would've been too much to try and patch up their lives in the middle of anticipating a baby. Legend himself had no worries, no stress and no reason at all to frown. If Sheena thought that he was goofy, loud and a grinning fool before, to know that through all of what they experienced Sheena didn't leave, he was more so all of his lively self because of her. Every other Saturday night at their new home was official Family Night.

All of his siblings and the rest of the Flockas would pile up there for games, foods and plenty of drinks. Legend was even looking into going to culinary school before opening his own restaurant. That would have to come after he held his beloved at gunpoint so that she would finally meet him at the altar.

The men left their backpacks in their rented SUV when they got out of it at the front of Ms. Jackson's shop. Most of the community had lined up down the block to get ready for the wedding that most of them had been waiting on.

Sheena helped Kalie out of a horse-drawn carriage while Mocha caught the end of her sister's long train so that it wouldn't drag on the ground just yet. Kalie couldn't keep her tears at bay from the time Queenie buttoned the last pearl button on her daughter's bodice. Her day was there. Every girl's fantasy. Sheena dabbed her sister's tears away with a piece of cloth so that Kalie wouldn't mess up her white, silver, and purple shadow. The makeup artist already had to go over her face twice because she couldn't stop crying.

Usually, it would've been dishonorable for a Haitian to marry while pregnant, however, Queenie didn't have a problem reminding elders that Kalie was Afro-Cuban.

As soon as Scrappy saw his bride in her all-white gown, he had to tear up on his own. Her bodice hosted a sweetheart neckline and pearls in intricate designs all over it. Her chiffon skirt flared at the hips and had a six-foot train behind it in ruffled layers.

Scrappy accepted a silver and purple sash from Ms. Jackson as his wedding gift; he adjusted it over his torso after she had handed it to him. Queenie placed a silver crown onto his head while Mocha was adjusting her sister's extravagant tiara. As soon as Scrappy's fingers intertwined with Kalie's, a jolt of electricity shot up his arm and settled into his spine. The moment felt so right. With Phara on the other side of him and her hand in his, Scrappy was very much so complete.

Sheena and Mocha grabbed up Kalie's train with Legend and Calmly behind them and Queenie in the middle. They were all ready to make their march down to the church to have the ceremony that brought tears to many eyes.

A tall, bronze skin man with light brown eyes stood on the porch of the church, dressed in white with a smile on his chiseled face. He took his hands from his pockets and stepped down the only four stairs of the church with a folded piece of paper in his hand. He presented to a shocked and misty-eyed Scrappy.

Scrappy accepted the page, unfolded it, and scanned it. He then looked up at his father. The sense of being overjoyed consumed him so much so that he had to wrap his arms around Xavier's shoulders.

"I had to come out of my feelings and out of my denial," Xavier told him in Creole. "That woman poisoned us a lot. In turn, I hurt you. We can't get back the time we lost, but we can start making beautiful memories... if you'll have me. I just know that I wasn't going to miss this moment from my only child and only son." Xavier pulled away from his son and looked down at such a beautiful granddaughter that he had never gotten the chance to know.

Scrappy composed himself well as he looked down at Xavier's honorable release form in his hand. Then, he looked over at Kalie, telling her, "Kay… baby, this is my father. Xavier Broadus."

A smile appeared on Kalie's face as her tears spilled over once more. She hugged him, having his lips to meet both her cheeks as a greeting. "I see how and why Edwin is so menacing but dashing."

"I try," he told her with a thick French accent. "Now, beautiful," he then said to Phara as he squatted before her. "What might interest you more? Getting to know your old grandfather, or having your mommy and daddy marry so we can go and party and dance?"

"Marry!" she cheered.

"Well, alright." Xavier picked her up and waited for Scrappy and Kalie to step aside so that he, Phara, and Queenie could enter first, then the rest of the wedding party before the couple of the hour.

For three hours, Scrappy and Kalie sat in facing chairs, listening to people from the community say honorable and beautiful things about Scrappy. Some of Queenie's girls, along with Sheena and Mocha, gave teary-eyed speeches and blessings for the union. Calmly and Legend took to the podium together to give their boy hell before he left, and there wasn't a settled stomach in the church from how hard the two had everyone laughing. Even Scrappy had to get out of his seat and clap a few times at their comedic punchlines about his life and how far he had come in love and in life. The breath-taker of them all was when Xavier decided to take the microphone, yet his speech wasn't as long as Queenie's or Ms. Jackson's.

He smoothed his hand over the sides of his wavy hair, making sure that there wasn't a strand out of place before his ponytail holder held his thick strands together in one long braid that stopped at his waist behind his back. With a trembling hand, he adjusted the mic to meet his six-five height, and then took his eyes to Kalie.

"Today, I give you my only son in hopes that you can make the rest of his days so pure and blissful; for I have contributed to the darkness of his past and the strength of his heart all the same. I pray that you include your traditions and help to make my son a better man, a better father, and that you are patient with him. I hope that you can be as flexible as a wife is supposed to be and become a much better asset than his own mother. Kalie, I've had opportunities to meet you, but I have not. Being in a mental state is dishonorable in our culture, so you see, I had to stay away. I apologize for secluding myself when my son needed me. But you see, he didn't need me. He needed you, Kalie. The love you have bestowed upon Edwin brings him such a light glow that I have never seen in my son. He is nothing like I remember, and I must thank you for helping to shape, mold, and bring something out of him that I'm sure neither of us thought existed anymore.

"To my son, I hope that you can forgive me. Even though you've said that you do, I only need ask once more on your special day, in order to allow me back into the family. I hope to know you as a man and father, my granddaughter, and my unborn grandchild. I hope to contribute every waking moment to this union because I have failed so miserably in the past. And as it is said in our culture, Edwin Broadus, the son of Xavier and Judeline Broadus, you may now leave home and collect your own. From a father's heart to his son's, I bless this union and wish you much peace, happiness, and longevity. Oh, and please don't forget that we don't believe in divorce, hence the reason your mother and I are still not on paper as a divorced couple. If you don't like Kalie in the morning, you're stuck, Chuck." Xavier winked at his son with a smile while the crowd died down from their tears and sniffles turned laughs and claps.

The finale of the three-hour ceremony was Kalie grazing the backs of her fingers over Scrappy's leathery cheek where his burn healed, and him kissing her exposed bullet wound. When the Reverend gave the okay after the vows, their lips came together to finally seal their promise of longevity of love, honor, and sacrifice.

"You're not going to get tired of me, are you?" Kalie asked just below the applause of the church full of people.

Scrappy smirked. "I'll always be your savage, ti kras fanm mwen. And you'll always have my heart."

"Good. Because my water just broke."

THE END

OTHER ROYAL RELEASES FROM SUNNY

Chosen: A Street King's Obsession (1 - 3)

Givana & Slay: A No Questions Asked Love Story

A Forbidden Street King's Love Story

A Forbidden Street King's Love Story 2:
Through Hell & High Water

Love & Cocaine: A Savage Love Story

Love & Cocaine 2: For Better or Worse

Stuck on You: Shane & Cherie's Story (1 - 4)

Obsessed with a Savage

Caught Between Two Street Kings

Her Savage His Heart: Loving a Miami Bully (1- 2)

CONNECT WITH SUNNY!

Twitter & Instagram: @imthatgiovanni

Tumblr: knojokegio.tumblr.com

Google Plus: Sunny Giovanni

Facebook: https://www.facebook.com/thesunnygiovanni/

Looking for a publishing home?

Royalty Publishing House, Where the Royals reside, is accepting submissions for writers in the urban fiction genre. If you're interested, submit the first 3-4 chapters with your synopsis to submissions@royaltypublishinghouse.com.

Check out our website for more information: www.royaltypublishinghouse.com.

Text ROYALTY to 42828 to join our mailing list!

To submit a manuscript for our review, email us at
submissions@royaltypublishinghouse.com

Text RPHCHRISTIAN to 22828 for our
CHRISTIAN ROMANCE novels!

Text RPHROMANCE to 22828 for our
INTERRACIAL ROMANCE novels!

Get LiT!

Download the LiTeReader app today and enjoy exclusive content, free books, and more

Do You Like CELEBRITY GOSSIP?

Check Out QUEEN DYNASTY!
Visit Our Site: www.thequeendynasty.com

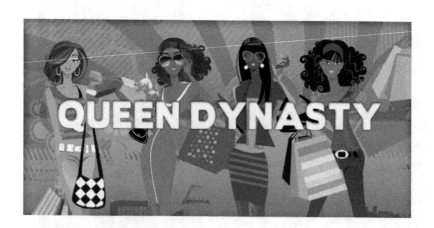

05802 3301

CPSIA information can be obtained
at www.ICGtesting.com
Printed in the USA
LVHW04s2302180518
577693LV00011B/699/P